On the stoop s‌ ‌ ‌
doing her best ‌‌ ‌‌
blue meringue in an oversize puffy
jacket.

A thick scarf was wound around her neck, covering her chin. On her head was jammed a woollen beanie. Strands of golden hair had escaped from its confines, drifting around her face. Even though she was wrapped up tight against the icy breeze, her cheeks had taken on a windblown pink and her nose glowed a cute rose red. She gripped a solid-looking rectangular case in one gloved hand and the rickety handle of a battered wheelie bag in the other.

A traveler. Who now offered him a faltering smile from her generously proportioned mouth, which lit the whole of her and turned "ordinary" into something luminous.

A distraction.

Stefano would have no distractions, not here. No angelic visions with pale skin, honey eyes and cherry lips. While other castles in Europe were open to the public, his family had resolutely refused to share this most private of spaces. Barely any photographs of the treasures here existed in the public domain. Once he'd thought that a waste. Now he saw it as a blessing—one that he would not have disturbed.

When **Kali Anthony** read her first romance novel at fourteen, she realized a few truths: there can never be too many happy endings, and one day she would write them herself. After marrying her own tall, dark and handsome hero in a perfect friends-to-lovers romance, Kali took the plunge and penned her first story. Writing has been a love affair ever since. If she isn't battling her cat for access to the keyboard, you can find Kali playing dress-up in vintage clothes, gardening, or bushwhacking with her husband and three children in the rain forests of South East Queensland.

Books by Kali Anthony

Harlequin Presents

Revelations of His Runaway Bride
Bound as His Business-Deal Bride
Off-Limits to the Crown Prince

Visit the Author Profile page
at Harlequin.com for more titles.

Kali Anthony

SNOWBOUND IN HIS BILLION-DOLLAR BED

HARLEQUIN®
PRESENTS®

Recycling programs
for this product may
not exist in your area.

ISBN-13: 978-1-335-56839-7

Snowbound in His Billion-Dollar Bed

Copyright © 2022 by Kali Anthony

All rights reserved. No part of this book may be used or reproduced in
any manner whatsoever without written permission except in the case of
brief quotations embodied in critical articles and reviews.

This is a work of fiction. Names, characters, places and incidents
are either the product of the author's imagination or are used fictitiously.
Any resemblance to actual persons, living or dead, businesses,
companies, events or locales is entirely coincidental.

This edition published by arrangement with Harlequin Books S.A.

For questions and comments about the quality of this book,
please contact us at CustomerService@Harlequin.com.

Harlequin Enterprises ULC
22 Adelaide St. West, 41st Floor
Toronto, Ontario M5H 4E3, Canada
www.Harlequin.com

Printed in U.S.A.

SNOWBOUND IN HIS BILLION-DOLLAR BED

To my darling aunt and godmother, Joanie, who gave me my first craft book on writing romance and told me to follow my dreams. They really did come true.

CHAPTER ONE

'YOU DON'T KNOW what you're talking about, Moretti.'

The man on the other end of the phone sounded full of bravado, but it was all an act. Stefano was conscious of every nuance in the voice. The heightened tone, the subtle tremor. And it was right that this worthless member of Lasserno's upper echelons should worry. Yet another thief of the country's treasures Stefano was intent on rooting out.

He settled back into the antique leather chair, which creaked underneath him. They all started out like this—with denial. And so far they'd all told the truth in the end. Liars. Every one of them. All about to fall from grace with a thud unless they gave him what he wanted.

He knew all about falls from grace. The landing was an uncompromising one. Stefano Moretti, Count of Varno, former private secretary to Lasserno's Prince Alessio Arcuri, had died on a hill of good intentions months ago. What had risen from those ashes was a man with a coal-dark heart, harder than black diamonds.

'My proper title is *Your Excellency*, but I'll ignore the slight.'

It reminded Stefano that word of his fall was now

more than a speculative whisper. Those who'd sought to cut him down were emboldened.

He let out a long, steadying breath. There was no time for this introspection. He had a job to do. Self-appointed, but an important role nonetheless. One that would protect his siblings, even though he might never be forgiven and would certainly never forgive himself for what he'd done.

Betrayal had no sweetener. Secretly reporting your monarch's private movements to the press tended to be a deal-breaker—particularly when you were said monarch's private secretary, most trusted confidant and best friend.

It didn't matter that his motives had been altruistic. The press had been grossly unfair to Alessio when he'd taken the throne after his father's abdication. It had caused fear and instability in Lasserno, which had already been suffering from the former Prince's excesses. All Stefano had suggested was using the press for good as successfully as Alessio's father had done for nefarious means. When Alessio had shunned the idea Stefano had taken matters into his own hands. Leaks about Alessio's private visit to Lasserno's Children's Hospital had been carefully dropped.

But what Stefano hadn't figured on was losing control of the beast. The press hadn't been satisfied with the scant crumbs he'd scattered for them and had scrabbled for more.

As good as his motives had been, he'd faced up to the consequences. Alessio had almost lost Hannah, his one-time portrait artist and now beloved Princess, because of Stefano's actions. It had ended well, with a marriage during Stefano's exile and a little prince or princess on the way soon. But, whilst there didn't appear to be any long-term harm, he accepted the need to pay a penance, possibly for as long as he lived…

'Let me refresh your memory on what I'm after.' Stefano stopped trying for a conciliatory tone and injected every shred of contempt he could find into each word. 'A diamond. Ten carats. Formerly from the Arcuri parure. Does that sound familiar? I've no doubt you'll remember, since Signor Giannotti reports that someone of your *exact* description tried selling it to him a week ago. As questionable as that man's honesty might be, he knows his gems. When he realised the stone came from the Crown Jewels, he called me immediately.'

Silence.

They all fell silent when they realised how far his reach still went. He had eyes everywhere and he wouldn't fail in this mission. His brother and sister relied on his success.

The Moretti family was inextricably linked to the Crown—a centuries-old obligation. One he'd blighted by his actions. He didn't want his siblings shackled to that now poisoned chalice. They should be able to leave Lasserno and find their own future. He'd promised them that freedom and he wouldn't deviate. Because his fall from grace could not stay secret indefinitely, and the country would see them as guilty by association. Already the rumours had reached their ears, impacting on their prospects. They'd reported being snubbed by some. Now he'd completed his degree in horticulture, Gino's employer was taking too long to provide a letter of endorsement to assure an introduction at Kew, where his brother dreamed of a role. Emilia's final months in teaching and early childhood seemed to be mired in an inordinate amount of paperwork, with no-one having the inclination to finalise it so she could take up a hoped-for placement overseas.

When his job was complete, he'd ask for his siblings to be released from the link to the royal family which would always hold him. Then they could do as they wished—he wouldn't allow his taint to spread over them like a slick of oil. He'd redeem the Moretti family name for their sakes. Stefano considered himself irredeemable.

'You think you're so clever,' rasped the disembodied voice on the other end of the line, 'but no one believes the palace's fairy-tale that you're on a sabbatical to restore your family castle.'

This was the official version. An innocuous press release to explain why Stefano was no longer seen in his role as Alessio's private secretary, when once he had always been at the Prince's side. A final act of grace from his former best friend and employer.

It was more than Stefano deserved for his betrayal.

'I don't care what people believe,' he said with disdain, when all he wanted to do was rage.

Stefano quelled that desire, doused the burn threatening to ignite and roar into life inside him. *Patience.* This was only the first part of his plan to free his siblings. He wouldn't be distracted from the task of recovering the precious gems Alessio's father had given away like meaningless trinkets in the months before his abdication.

His second task, however, was proving far more difficult. Some might say unachievable...

'The many artisans clamouring to work on Castello Varno's restoration would say otherwise.'

Often the biggest lies were hidden behind small truths.

His work for Alessio had kept him in the capital, and his siblings hadn't paid much attention to the state of the castle. Gino and Emilia were tangled up in their own dreams of the future he'd promised them when he'd taken on the role of their protector as a teenager, since his parents had had little interest in the younger children.

Even though they knew he would always take their calls, his brother had thought him far too busy to worry about some stones crumbling from the ramparts in the unused reaches of their home. Likewise, his sister hadn't thought about the maintenance of the central heating, which seemed irrelevant in a mild summer, but critical when winter arrived in force.

Perhaps he should have shared with them what it truly took to run the castle. Being head of the family since his father's death four years earlier, he viewed their ancestral home as his personal responsibility. And, whilst he might have disgraced the Moretti name, he would not let the castle which had dominated the mountains of this northern province of Lasserno for five hundred years fall into ruin. He was still the Count, even if he no longer deserved the title.

'A pretty little bird tells me you have your own problems,' the other man said, as if trying to regain some of the ground rapidly sliding away from him.

The words found their mark, straight and true.

Stefano shut his eyes. *Celine*. What was one more arrow of pain embedded in his heart when he'd already taken so many? She must be the one to have started the rumours because Alessio would say nothing, of that Stefano had no doubt.

When he'd taken the honourable route and resigned from his position, he'd believed Celine would understand. They'd been together for five years, engaged for three, and were planning a future—a dynastic marriage of their own.

A member of Lasserno's aristocracy, Celine had professed her love for him soon after they'd begun dating. Smiled with apparent joy when he'd proposed. They'd planned to wed after Alessio was crowned... Yet their break-up had followed fast on the heels of Stefano's resignation and return to Varno. He couldn't forget her final words, now a poisonous and constant voice in his ear.

'You're nothing, Stefano, if you're not working for the Prince.'

All those years she'd whispered that he was better than the role of private secretary. That he should ask Alessio for something of greater prestige, as if his centuries-old title as the Count of Varno wasn't enough. He hadn't cared at the time, since helping his friend navigate the abdication and the financial mire into which his father had plunged Lasserno had been vital work.

Yet Celine had been right. The moment he stood on unstable ground the vultures had circled, fighting to fill the void with their refusal to take his phone calls, their quiet disdain not only of him but of his brother and sister, who didn't deserve similar contempt.

The brutal ache of realisation burrowed deep. One of the few people he'd thought he could trust had not kept his devastating secret. But, as he well knew, information was currency, and news of his downfall would be more fodder for the aristocratic rumour mill. Celine was only protecting herself from being tarnished by association, making herself queen of the gossip circle at his expense. Anyhow, he had no cause to expect anything else, since he'd betrayed his best friend. In that act he'd shown that no one could really be trusted—most of all himself.

Celine had been right to walk away on her towering heels, without a backward glance. He was not worthy of forgiveness. Disgraced. Untrustworthy. What good was he to anyone now? She'd made that brutally clear. In those final moments of their relationship any hope and all expectation of how his life would play out in front of him had withered and died.

Stefano gripped his phone till the edges cut into his fingers. Whilst his problems were entirely self-inflicted, he didn't have to lie down and allow himself to be kicked.

'You shouldn't listen to pretty little birds. They may sing a lovely song, but all they're doing is distracting you from the raptor in the clouds above. I sharpen my talons each night. Don't think you'll escape my grip when I clasp you tight.'

When he was successful, his mission would allow him to walk into the royal palace with his head held high, rather than slither back on his belly like the snake he'd become. He had nothing left to him but the merest splinter of pride, and he would *not* lose that as well.

'You have no evidence bar the words of a known criminal.'

'I have CCTV,' Stefano replied. 'I have Signor Giannotti's signed statement. I have enough.'

A choking kind of sound was all that came down the line, followed by a few more moments of silence.

'His Highness *gave* it to me.'

Ah. The whining. Lies first…bargaining second. The pattern was familiar and sickening. Anger tended to come third, and Stefano was spoiling for a fight.

'The former Prince may have given it to you. The current Prince wants it back. You had no right to keep it. That diamond is the country's, not yours.'

Which wasn't entirely true. Being the principality's absolute monarch meant the Prince or Princess could do anything they pleased.

Cold like a block of glacial ice settled in Stefano's gut. So long as Gino and Emilia were protected, he would take whatever came his way. He tried not to think of what his future might hold…of the unopened letters in his desk from the palace and the calls he'd ignored. Not yet. Because they signalled nothing good. His attentions must be fixed on the task at hand. He wanted no more pleading. Weasel words sickened him. People should own their actions and make reparation before seeking forgiveness. Nothing else was acceptable.

'Here's what will happen,' he said. 'You'll return the diamond to the palace and all will be forgotten.'

Stefano was in no place to make that promise, but

so be it. He didn't care so long as it got him what he wanted.

'If you don't, I will storm down upon you like an avalanche from the mountains and you *will* be crushed in my wake. Nothing will remain, I promise you.'

'It…it may take some time.'

There it was. The capitulation. These people were weak. If you stripped the meat from all of them you'd barely have enough bones to make one spine. At least his family's centuries-old role as Shield of the Crown was still good for something other than the burden it imposed. He should have made more of it. Fought Alessio for what he believed was right rather than let it go and make the fateful decision to go to the press.

But he could indulge in disgust at his personal failings sometime later, when this job was done.

'Since I'm a generous man, I'll give you two days. Only remember. My eyes are everywhere. There is not a jeweller, pawnbroker, thief or fence in Europe who doesn't know about the missing stones and all are looking for them at my request. Two days.'

He disconnected. Tossed his mobile on the desk, where it landed with a clatter on the burnished wood. Talking to these thieves and fools left him in need of a shower. He might be soiled by his personal actions, but he'd never be as grubby as them, stealing the nation's heritage.

Stefano stood and walked to the window, staring out at the last of the melting snow. Spring was overdue, and winter not keen to relinquish her grip this year. Luckily he'd sent any remaining staff back to their homes a few days earlier, with the weather reports and a glowering sky hinting that more snow was on its way. The castle's aged heating, not coping of late, left most of the building's rooms with an unforgiving chill. There was no point in his staff being trapped in the cold too.

They'd worried about him, being alone here, but he'd only opened few rooms since his return, and he'd assured them he was perfectly capable of looking after himself.

Anyhow, it didn't matter if the unseasonal mountain weather cut him off from the rest of Lasserno. He'd been cut off from the country ever since that fateful day he'd announced his betrayal to Alessio and handed in his resignation, returning to Castello Varno, where he hadn't set foot for three years. Still, though his current work wasn't officially sanctioned, he'd continue until he was done. Stefano wasn't about to allow his brother and sister to suffer any more for his sins.

Time spent gazing out of the window wouldn't solve those problems. Stefano returned to his well-worn chair, his computer. He glanced at the half-full bottle of grappa sitting on the desk in front of him. Many like it had kept him company over the long, cold winter here. A shot of that would keep him warm for the next few hours as he worked. He grabbed a glass. Poured a solid measure into it. He took a hefty gulp which wouldn't have done justice to a finer blend, but this local version was more moonshine than anything else.

The burn of it heated him from the inside out, fortifying him for the long night of work ahead. Stefano needed to spend some time on the second part of his plan to ensure that his brother and sister were protected.

An almost impossible task, yet one which would yield the greatest reward for his siblings.

'If you can find the Heart of Lasserno I'll give you anything you want.'

A promise from a prince to a friend.

Back then, with an arrogance which should have sounded a warning of his future failings, Stefano had joked about being made Prime Minister. He and Alessio had both been younger and less world-weary then, trying to make their mark. What better way than finding the Heart of Lasserno—their country's coronation ring—lost since it had been handed over to a foreign soldier for protection in the desperate dying days of World War II?

If he recovered the jewels, and if he found the ring, it would cement his position once more. He'd be able to walk back into the palace, his family's reputation safe and assured, and respond to whatever command his monarch might make with some pride left.

But there he'd hit a wall built by time.

Stefano opened the document his investigator had emailed to him. Read it. No matter how much money he burned trying to find that Australian soldier, all he had was an unlikely amalgam of a name. Art Cacciatore. A man who'd ceased to exist—if he'd ever existed at all.

Stefano glanced at the half-empty glass on his desk. Tempting as it was to drown his sorrows, now was a time for work. He'd drink the castle's cellar dry in celebration when his job was done.

The investigator's report held no further joy for him so he left his desk. Approached an armchair near the fire crackling in a marble fireplace, readying himself for the seemingly endless chore of trawling through dusty boxes of family records for any useful information. The weight of the task, the exhaustion, the self-recrimination—all threatened to crush him. But this was not about his feelings. He wasn't in the practice of granting sympathy for self-inflicted wounds.

As he sat down, a distant chime rang out. The doorbell? Perhaps the local village mechanic and handyman, Bruno, had finally decided to risk the weather and come to assess the castle's heating, as he'd promised to do for the past week.

Stefano rose and left his office, rubbing his arms against the bracing temperature away from the fire. He made his way to the entrance hall past rooms shut down when his mother had left to live in an apartment in Lasserno's capital after his father had died. The whole place looked as unlived-in as it had since he'd returned here all those months ago in self-imposed exile.

The bell chimed again. Loud, strident this time, as if someone had leaned on it.

'Sì, sì. Sto arrivando!'

He reached the entrance foyer, undid the ancient locks, which groaned in icy protest, and hauled the front door open to a blast of frigid air.

Not Bruno.

On the steps stood a woman doing her best to mimic a pale blue meringue in an oversized puffy jacket, zipped up high. A thick scarf wound round her neck, covering her chin. On her head was jammed a woollen hat, replete with polar bear patterns and pom-poms. Strands of golden hair had escaped from its confines, drifting round her face. Even though she was wrapped up tight against the icy breeze her cheeks had taken on a windblown pink and her nose glowed a cute rose-red. She gripped a solid-looking rectangular case in one gloved hand, and the rickety handle of a battered wheelie bag in another.

A traveller. Who now offered him a faltering smile from her generously proportioned mouth which lit the whole of her and turned 'ordinary' into something luminous.

A distraction.

He would have no distractions—not here. No angelic visions with pale skin, honey eyes and cherry lips. Whilst other castles in Europe were open to the public, his family had resolutely refused to share this most private of spaces. Barely any photographs of the treasures here existed in the public domain. Once he'd thought it a waste. Now he saw it as a blessing—one which he would not have disturbed.

'Niente turisti,' he said, perhaps a little emphatically.

Those honey eyes widened and she took a step back, her mouth opening in a perfectly drawn *O* accompanied by what sounded like a squeak…like a little mouse in his doorway. Except her eyes were not the eyes of a mouse. They flashed tiger-gold.

'C-Count Moretti? Your Excellency? I don't speak Italian. *Non parlo It—*'

'No tourists,' he repeated, in English now, given his initial oversight. The words rasped out of him and he cleared his throat. It had been so long he'd almost forgotten how to engage in polite conversation. Not that he felt particularly polite in this moment. The internet and guidebooks, if anyone still used them, were quite clear. 'The castle does not take tourists.'

Her shoulders drooped, and then she seemed to collect herself. Straightened. 'I'm not a tourist. I'm Lucille Jamieson.'

She said the words in a broad accent that was neither English nor North American, as if she had every expectation that he knew who she was.

'You're not from here.'

'No, I'm Australian. But—'

'Then you *are* a tourist and you have travelled a long way for nothing.'

'I'm working in Salzburg right now, so only about fourteen hours' drive away, and—'

'Not from Lasserno—ergo, a tourist.'

He crossed his arms. Her golden gaze followed the move and a pleasant warmth seemed to glow in his chest, a balm against the cold outside. Clearly the grappa was finally doing its job. He might even be able to remove his sweater soon.

He ran his finger around the neck. Its wool was suddenly overheating him, even in the bitter breeze.

The woman—*Lucille*—bit into her plump bottom lip. That warm glow inside him ignited and caught fire. Those perfect white teeth were torturing her delicate flesh. He saw how it blanched a pale rose, then flushed into something darker. It must sting, what she was doing... How he'd like to soothe it for her...

'I sent a letter. Since you don't have a public email... which is very old school and kind of like my grandfather was...but I suppose you do live in a castle.'

His head spun at the tumble of words spilling from

her unchecked, but he understood one of them loud and clear. Had she said he was like her *grandfather*? Something about that comparison punctured an ego he hadn't realised he still possessed. Stefano couldn't understand the sensation at all. She looked young and, sure, at thirty-one he might be a little bit older. But why did it matter to him?

He didn't dwell on it. She wouldn't be here long enough for him to need to, or care.

'I have received no letter, Signorina Jamieson.' Though a small stack of mail, including some official and ignored pieces of correspondence from the palace, *did* sit in a drawer of his desk. He was waiting for an opportune time to open them, because pieces of correspondence like that never contained good news... 'You must leave. There's a *pensione* in the village where you can stay.'

A flurry of snow fell behind her, soft and white. The narrow roads here would soon become treacherous for anyone inexperienced in driving on them.

He'd loved snow as a child, until he'd realised the danger when you didn't pay careful attention. If he hadn't found Emilia that dark night long ago, when she'd run away to catch a last glimpse of their mother in her fairy-tale gown on the way to yet another ball, he'd have lost his younger sister for ever...

That was the moment he decided that if his parents weren't going to care for his siblings, he had to.

'I'm booked in there, but there's been some mix-up and they aren't ready for me. The owner told me to go sightseeing for a while, and drive towards the castle since they knew I was looking to come here...eventually.'

Her mouth began to tremble now, but her eyes remained clear and warm. No hint of tears. He'd know if there were. Celine had given him enough whenever she hadn't got her own way for him to recognise the early signs. Signorina Jamieson's shoulders had slumped again, like a plant wilting for lack of water. Then her gaze drifted behind him with a look almost like pain. Her eyes wide with longing.

'Please. M-my car b-broke down. I've w-walked a l-long way and it's s-started s-snowing.'

Her teeth were chattering. This woman, Lucille Jamieson, was cold, and he knew how dangerous hypothermia was if it set in. He gritted his teeth, a curdle of dissatisfaction stewing in his gut. No matter how little he wanted this stranger in his home, he couldn't send her away with no transport. He had no choice.

Stefano stepped back and gestured behind him, beckoning her in. 'The broken-down car should have been where you *started* our conversation.'

She stood seemingly frozen on the doorstep, framed as a bright, vibrant splash against the grey and white world behind her. Her eyes widened, her gaze slowly tracking down his body. All of him tightened at her thorough perusal.

'Y-you confuse me,' she said.

'There is no confusing my invitation. Come in.'

The inertia that had gripped her slowly lifted and she half wheeled, half dragged her bag over the threshold. She hadn't moved far when it listed to one side and the wheel fell off with an undignified clatter on the mosaic floor. She looked at it, and let out a noise almost like a whimper.

That small, defeated sound tugged at something inside of him he'd thought long dead. A shred of empathy.

He sighed. Reached out his hand. 'Let me take that.'

Then at least he could get her in front of the fire and start to thaw her out. Her lips had taken on an alarming bluish tinge, almost the same frigid colour of her travesty of a jacket. Not that he had been staring at her lips again. It was normal concern, that was all.

In response, she dropped the handle of the wheelie bag, but clutched the other case tight to her body as if it held the Crown Jewels. 'Thank you. I'll carry this one.'

He shrugged, shut the door on the rapidly plummeting temperature behind them and grabbed her bulging suitcase. Whilst he considered himself strong enough—he was spending more time than usual in his gym of late, when he couldn't sleep—even he could tell this luggage required an excess baggage warning.

'*Dio*, what do you keep in here?'

'Oh, you know…' She shrugged. Her windblown cheeks darkened, her gaze darting around the space. 'Crucifix. Garlic. Wooden stakes.'

Stefano tensed. He dropped the bag back to the floor, where it landed with an impressive thud. 'You're carrying *what*?'

She gave a trilling kind of laugh which sounded as musical as it did nervous.

Who *was* this woman? Someone who wrote him letters and drove to his castle in an impending snowstorm. He might almost be concerned, except standing here, in this vast entrance hall, Lucille Jamieson didn't appear to pose any threat. She simply looked sad and somehow…*crushed*.

He was overcome by the inexplicable need to hunt down and conquer whatever had wounded her.

'Look, I've driven a long number of hours straight to get here. Now I'm in a creepy castle with a man who's a count. Tell me this doesn't sound *exactly* like a horror movie.'

'You were making a joke. Of course.' Stefano relaxed a fraction. After a few days alone his imagination seemed to be running as wild as hers. 'But the castle is not *creepy*.'

He took umbrage at the assertion. *Uncompromising* might be one description. *Imposing* an even better word.

Signorina Jamieson's gaze darted around the expansive entrance hall, with its forbidding paintings of former Counts covering the walls.

'Those pictures are all of judgemental-looking people wearing black. I'd describe the vibe as...*funereal*.' Her voice was almost a whisper, and she bit into her lip again, which thankfully had some colour returning to it.

'My father said it was a statement of intent to any who entered.'

'Well, it doesn't exactly scream *warm welcome*.'

Her eyes were big and wide. Every part of her appeared stiff and tense, especially the way she still clutched her remaining case to her, as if in self-protection.

'I can't promise there aren't more pictures of my disapproving ancestors throughout my home, but I *can* promise I'm no creature of the night. You're welcome here.' The lie about her being welcome slipped easily enough from his tongue. He had no desire to terrify a stranded woman. 'Please follow me.'

'Thank you.'

'*Prego*. Lasserno's hospitality is renowned. I intend to uphold those traditions.'

Now he needed to make a decent attempt at showing her some of the hospitality he professed to have. Stefano headed through the entrance hall towards the living area. The heated prickling at the back of his neck told him the woman was close on his heels.

After a few minutes of walking through the cold, deserted halls, he opened the door to a room which had been the playroom of his childhood. When Stefano had relocated from the capital and begun full-time residence at the castle, he'd taken over the space and moved some of the more comfortable furniture inside. The memories here, at least, were fond ones. Of spending time with his siblings even though they'd been younger and at the time it had seemed like an imposition, being left to care for them with a neglectful nanny.

The rest of the castle was meant as a showcase for his family's might and power in the province of Varno. Designed to impress, inspire awe. In this room, where he'd spent so much of his time, he always felt as if he'd come home.

He deposited Signorina Jamieson's weighty bag inside the door, walked to the fire and carefully placed more fuel on the low-burning coals. Prodded it until the flames blazed brighter.

The woman in question stood at the entrance to the room as if she was taking it all in, then she raked off her hat. A spill of strawberry blonde tresses fell about her shoulders, unruly and golden. She looked as if she'd recently been tumbled into bed with her mussed-up hair and her rosy cheeks…

But his role here was not harbouring illicit thoughts about stray tourists. And it didn't seem she had similar opinions about him. She didn't pay much attention to him at all, instead hesitating, then looking down at her mud-splattered footwear.

A frown crinkled her brow. 'I'm sorry. My boots really are a mess. I should have taken them off.'

Everything about her seemed uncertain. Tentative. Even her comments about spooky castles and counts and horror movies. Was she afraid? He'd never frightened a woman—ever. On the contrary, once he'd known how to be gentle and kind. How to exhibit care. His official designation—Shield of the Crown—meant he was a protector. As little as he wanted her here, that instinct was ingrained. He'd try to put her at ease until he could safely have her collected and returned to the village.

'There's no need for an apology. You can take off your boots in a moment. Please sit.'

The way she swayed on her feet made him believe she might fall over, and he had no desire to catch a swooning female. To clasp that soft, curved weight in his arms. To feel the way her head might nestle in the crook of his shoulder, her breath feathering his neck as he carried her to the couch…

No. They were things he wished to avoid, even though the thought made him delectably warm. Or perhaps it was merely the fire. That must be it, since he was still crouched close, tending the flames.

She finally made her way to the couch nearest to the fireplace, resting the black case she still held gently beside her, settling it into the cushions, ensuring it was steady. Then she tugged at her laces and kicked off her boots. Her feet were encased in woolly blue socks with a polar bear pattern that matched her hat. She pointed her toes in the direction of the fire and wiggled them.

Then she pulled the gloves from her hands, exposing slender fingers, and flexed them, before digging the thumb of her right hand deep into her left palm. Something about her seemed too fragile and soft. A strange contrast in this place where the past months had been all too hard. He wondered what had brought her here…what made her seem as if a part of her carried a mortal wound.

Stefano grabbed the fluffy blanket that his housekeeper had insisted would add an ambience to the room, for reasons which he found inexplicable, and held it out to her.

She took it and wrapped it round herself. 'Why is it still so cold in here?'

'The heating's been unpredictable. I'm waiting for Bruno, the local mechanic, to come and repair it.'

'He's the man I was talking to at the *pensione*. Who suggested that I come here.'

Of that, Stefano had no doubt. Bruno's wife ran the *pensione*. Bruno would have thought it a great joke, sending someone Stefano's way. Especially a young tourist who claimed not to be a tourist.

She leaned forward again, stretching her hands towards the fire now. He couldn't help but witness the small tremor running through her fingers.

'Ugh, I hate winter.'

Stefano had an intense desire to apologise, as if he

were personally responsible for Lasserno's unseasonal cold snap. He ignored it. 'I'll call Bruno and ask him to tow your car. Come and collect you and return you to the *pensione*.'

'The car's a rental.' She stared into the crackling fire, the light of it flickering golden across her pale face. 'I guess I need to talk to the company.'

'If you give me their name, Bruno will deal with them. If they give him any problems, they can deal with me.'

She withdrew her arms from in front of her and wrapped them round her waist, then turned to him and smiled. It was as if a hundred candles had been lit in the room, the brightness of her in this moment. The crinkles at the corners of her eyes. The way her beautiful mouth turned upwards, showing white teeth.

She was looking at him as if he were the solution to her every problem. But he was *not* that man. He never would be again. And yet the faith she showed in that fleeting, perfect moment made the blackened heart he'd thought had ceased to beat, stutter to life again.

'My grandfather was right about Lasserno's hospitality.'

'He travelled here?'

'That's what I tried to say in my letter. He was a navigator in World War II, on the run after his plane came down. He crossed the border from Italy to Lasserno. I—I believe your family might have taken him in till he could get back to his squadron?'

Stefano stilled. It was as if with her earlier smile the universe might have smiled down on him as well. But it was then that he noticed how drawn she appeared. A bluish tint under her eyes giving them a bruised quality. He shouldn't press. He should give her a hot drink and food, in the greatest of Lasserno's traditions. But it was as if every solution to his problems might rest in this one exhausted traveller, and he needed answers now. They would inform his next move.

'What was his name?' Stefano tried not to appear too eager. 'We kept some records, but many were lost when the enemy occupied our castle. Our country tried neutrality and was still drawn in.'

'Arthur Hunter. His friends used to call him Art. Did your family ever mention him?'

'That isn't a name that immediately comes to mind.'

Hunter… Hunter… His great-grandfather had written of a man, never forgetting promises made of taking a precious treasure to safety through the underground as the enemy were beating down the castle's door.

Could it be this easy? Stefano didn't know of an Arthur Hunter, but the English translation of *cacciatore* was "hunter". In the war, with language barriers, perhaps he had been given a name which was easily understood. Or perhaps he'd used the name as a joke, trying to hide himself all along.

But one thing was certain. Lucille Jamieson would not be returning to the *pensione* in the village. No. She would be staying here until he had the answers he sought.

CHAPTER TWO

LUCY TRIED TO get comfortable in the astonishing room, with its silk-lined walls, golden accents and frescoes on the ceiling. Even though the couch cushions were plush and deep, easy enough to sink into and never want to leave, it was hard to feel at ease with the Count of Varno…*looming.*

He was a man who looked as if he belonged in a gothic movie. Days-old stubble that on anyone else might have looked unkempt but on this man, added to his *film noir* appeal. He was tall, imposing, with a shock of thick black hair. Eyes so dark and piercing it was as if they had no pupils as he stared at her in an unblinking kind of way. *Glowered* at her, really. And, whilst she might have been frozen to the marrow, one look like that from him and she went up in flames.

When he'd first opened the door of this castle which rose ominously out of the mountainside, her instincts had told her to run. Slabs of gloomy grey stone… Turrets spearing from the solid base… Windows like the Count's dark judgemental eyes, piercing the sides of the structure.

But those instincts had let her down so poorly in recent months that she hadn't trusted them. So she'd kept on standing there, weak with exhaustion and the recognition that she was going nowhere on foot in the snow.

She liked to think she could be sensible about some things, even if the thought of walking into a castle that really did look like it belonged in a horror film had filled her with dread. But the truth was she had nowhere else to go. Her life in Salzburg, imploding. Australia, no haven either. Lasserno held answers to questions she didn't want to ask, but was being forced to, nonetheless.

Her grandfather had filled her head with stories of the kindness of the country's people to him during the war. It was a place he'd been over three-quarters of a century before and had never forgotten, although in his final days his memories had been fractured and consumed with guilt. He'd become obsessed by his culpability for some unnamed sin, which had been upsetting to both her and her mother, trying to comfort him without knowing the reason for his distress.

Still, she hoped his fond recollections of Lasserno had meant something, as all she craved right now was a bit of kindness. It was why she'd thrown everything she could fit into a single suitcase, turned her back on her life, and fled.

She closed her eyes, trying to shut out the thoughts that filled her head of those last days in Austria. Walking into her flat a little earlier than normal, finding her boyfriend, Viktor—

'My apologies, Signorina Jamieson. You've travelled a long way and must be tired.'

That voice of his stroked over her skin, all midnight and black velvet. She shivered—and not from the cold.

All she wanted to do was lean back in the seat and listen to him speak. Bask in the rich allure of his voice and let it wash over her like water from a hot bath. But, as tempting as that seemed, it was all just fantasy, at a time when she'd been forced to swallow a hefty dose of reality.

Sadly, reality was overrated.

She opened her eyes again.

'Thank you, Count Moretti. Or is it Your Excellency? I tried researching the correct form of address on the internet and I don't want to get it wrong.'

'There is no need for titles, *signorina*. Please call me Stefano.'

'Oh… Okay… And you can call me Lucy.'

Calling him by his first name seemed too intimate—as if some essential barrier between them had become shaky, turning into a kind of crumbling foundation that she really wanted to shore up with every bit of scaffolding she could find. But demanding more formality would be rude, and she hoped that here, in this castle, she might get the answers she searched for. Because it was that quest which now kept her glued to the seat.

That, and exhaustion. She was pretty sure her legs wouldn't move now, after walking as far as she had uphill, since the rental car she could ill afford had given an undignified lurch, a bang, and promptly died.

The corner of the Count's mouth hitched in a kind of smile, and the panic that had been churning around her stomach settled into something less like a hive of bees and more like a kaleidoscope of butterflies.

'*Lucy.*'

Her name sounded wonderful when said by him.

Special. Important in a way that had been lost to her years ago.

'What else did you research on the internet?'

She'd researched *him*. She wasn't a complete flake—even if this ill-fated and underprepared trip suggested otherwise. Any limited English language press showed Stefano Moretti in the background of photographs, behind Lasserno's Prince. Always looking sharp in dark sunglasses. More like a bodyguard than the private secretary those same press reports said was his job when he wasn't restoring his own castle.

The Count of Varno's official-looking website had plenty of information about his illustrious history and the Moretti family's proud links to the Crown, as if anything else about them was meaningless. The photograph of him there was a formal study in an exquisitely tailored suit. Tamed black hair. Shaved jaw sharp enough to cut glass. Undoubtedly a handsome man, yet the bland image was almost like a photo of a waxwork dummy.

This man in front of her was something more. Not restrained, perfectly pressed and two-dimensional, but bristling and alive, with the look of someone untamed. Almost feral.

A man she was now staring at, with the firelight flickering over his imposing form, making him appear like the king of the underworld, lording it over his minions…

But she really needed to stop these fevered kinds of fantasies. He was just a man. She was just a woman.

Somehow that realisation just made it worse.

And she still hadn't answered his question.

The Count of Varno—*Stefano*—raised one perfect black eyebrow. He stared at her cold and hard for a few moments and she wanted to blurt out all her secrets then and there. *Everything.*

But if she started it could take a while. A *long* while. She had no idea how he'd respond, given some of those secrets involved his family. Until she could figure out what his reaction might be, silence was her best friend.

'Oh, you know… Lasserno. The history of the Varno province.' *You.* But she didn't say that. She simply shrugged and hoped that covered the rest.

'I hope you will find Lasserno worthy of the visit.'

She hoped so too. Everything about her life lay in tatters around her. She needed answers—and they started in a family past she hadn't dwelled on much since her school days, when she'd had to write an essay on someone heroic and had written about her grandfather.

Lucy swallowed down the knot in her throat. Blinked away the sting in her eyes. She'd loved her granddad, and she missed him, wished she could ask him the truth about his history. But he'd passed away after a long life months earlier, and his death had left questions she had no answers to.

She wasn't sure now whether he was the hero she'd always thought him or the villain in a bigger tale. She hoped for the former, but the evidence suggested otherwise. It hurt almost worse than Viktor's betrayal, because Lucy was in desperate need of at least one man in her life to *stay* a good man when the rest had let her down.

'I'm sure your country will live up to its expectations.' Or at least she prayed it would.

Their eyes locked and somehow she forgot about the bone-deep cold that she'd thought would never leave her. Her cheating ex… The uncertainty of her position at work… How everything about her life that she'd thought solid had proved its foundation to be unstable…

There really was only her and him and the fire that cracked and popped in the huge marble fireplace beside her.

Then he blinked, broke the moment. Looked out of the window to the steady fall of snow outside. Whatever had passed between them was lost but she'd felt it—those fleeting seconds when all her focus had been on the present and not on what had gone before or might come next.

If only she could live in that blissful 'now' for ever. But her recent past was a mess and her impending future was bearing down on her with the terror and fury of a bear roaring out of the woods. She only hoped that she could put the broken pieces of her life back together.

'I'm forgetting myself,' he said, his voice a rough burr over her skin. 'Would you like a hot drink? Something to eat?'

'Please…' She'd eaten little in the past twenty-four hours, snatching food at service centres on the long drive from Salzburg to Lasserno. She really hadn't had the stomach for anything other than her escape.

'I've sent my staff back to their homes, given the snow warnings. And, whilst I can vouch for my beverage-making skills, the food will be simple.'

They were alone here? She tried not to think about it.

Surely he'd call the man in the village and get him to collect her? Then she'd arrange an appropriate time to talk—one when she'd look less waif and more like the capable woman she usually was, wearing the only nice dress she'd packed. Not muddy and unkempt…a damsel in distress needing rescue.

This was not the way her journey to the mountains of Lasserno was supposed to begin after she'd fled her home of the past twelve months. At twenty-four, she'd forged a career as one of the youngest orchestra leaders of the day. A girl from Down Under making it big as principal violinist in Europe… She should be proud of her achievements… But her life had unceremoniously unravelled before her and all she'd been able to do was watch in horror as it had careened out of control.

Yet again the sting of tears threatened. But these weren't tears of sadness—they were tears of anger. She blinked them away. There was no chance of her cheating jerk of an ex, Viktor, being granted any more tears. Not. A. Single. One. She couldn't have known that he'd also been spreading rumours to orchestra management about her niggling strain injury, which had led to the suggestion that she take some time away 'to consider her future'. Then her parents' relationship had finally fallen apart after one too many of her father's outrages. And now Lucy couldn't shake the sensation that every part of her life was a fraud.

No. Those thoughts weren't intruding again. The only fraud here was the travesty of the car she'd really not been able to afford to rent, so had found the cheapest option. Paying to keep her mother afloat after she'd finally left Lucy's dad, paying even more for solicitors so her father wouldn't steal everything her mother had built from her own career, had stripped Lucy financially. Lucy had become embroiled as well, with her father's solicitors saying the violin she played should form part of the financial pool in the wash-up of her parents' failed marriage. They'd claimed her mother had never given ownership of the centuries-old violin to Lucy, instead only loaning it to her.

And, to top it all off, she might be stuck here in a large, spooky castle with a man she didn't know. A man who still looked at her as if she was an unwelcome oddity dropped on his doorstep.

'I should ask… Do you have any likes, dislikes, allergies?'

That shred of thoughtfulness almost undid her. No one had thought of her much at all in the past months of what had turned into a bitter Austrian winter.

She shook her head. 'I don't eat brains or tripe.'

Stefano raised an eyebrow. She wanted to bury her head in her hands. She had no idea what caused her to ramble like this in front of him. It would be no surprise if he sent her back out into the snow.

Lucy tried to sound like someone who had control over her life and a working social filter. She even gave him what she hoped was a thankful smile. 'Whatever you have will be wonderful.'

He nodded and walked to the door. She could stare unabashed now at his broad shoulders, lovingly covered by the dark navy woollen sweater. At the glorious vee of his torso which spoke of consistent effort and strength. She really had no time for men with all the focus on her career. If asked, she'd say she was generally attracted to less hard-looking males, but in Stefano, Lucy was coming to realise the allure of testosterone-fuelled magnificence. Because 'magnificent' was the only adjective that really suited this man. He was almost dizzying with it.

The door shut behind him with the soft click of well-oiled hinges and she turned to the solid case beside her, designed to protect the precious contents within, which she always kept close.

Her violin.

She'd worried about it in the rapidly chilling weather. The instrument needed to be kept warm, like her. Treated with all the care such centuries-old wood deserved.

With her mother's own performing career in a string ensemble long ended, her mum had given Lucy the violin. The violin's history was almost as precious as the instrument itself, because it had saved her grandfather's life during the Second World War. He'd disguised his true identity as part of a downed allied flight crew by hiding as a violinist, playing in a band. No one had questioned the entertainers, and he'd travelled to safety with an instrument that was supposed to have been a reward for some heroic deeds—or so the family story had gone.

All lies.

This violin that she credited with her success was *far* more than an old and valuable piece of her family's tapestry. Everyone who knew anything about music commented on what an uncommon instrument it was, with its magnificent tone. Her grandfather had claimed it was a reproduction, no matter what the worn label inside might say. Still valuable because of its age and the expertise with which it had been made, was the only reason her father was trying to get his greedy hands on it. He'd ultimately stolen everything else of value from his family—why not this as well?

It was only when her mum had finally begun cleaning out Lucy's grandfather's house after his death, going through the diaries and papers packed tight into an old suitcase under the bed, that she'd discovered that what Lucy held in her hands at each concert, and played with love as an extension of her body and soul, was no copy. It was real.

A Stradivarius.

Lucy unclipped the travelling case with trembling fingers to check, but the violin lay safe and undamaged on the black velvet inside. After her mother's call, she'd been almost afraid to touch the instrument again. And even more terrifying than the knowledge that this violin was almost priceless was the reality that her grandfather hadn't been given it, but that it had been…*taken*.

Lucy had brought copies of certain diary entries with her—what her mother had managed to go through so far in her grief. Neat script written in wartime, when her grandfather had feared he wouldn't make it. Mention of some woman, Betty, was all wound up with talk of his time in Lasserno and then on the run. Parts, almost a coded chronicle for his family if he didn't survive, or that was what she thought.

It was as if by reading it she was learning something new about the gentle, caring man she'd talked with for hours about life and love. Whom she'd written to as she'd travelled overseas because he'd loved her postcards and letters. She'd adored him as a role model and a good man, because her father had always failed them.

Although now she recognised that the family had been given a sanitised version of his past before. The diaries told a story that was far darker and murkier. Of love, desperation and theft in wartime.

The violin is Lasserno's heart, not mine...

One thing seemed plain. Her grandfather had been given something priceless to protect by a family—most likely Stefano's family—and had kept it for his own. Fleeing with it to save himself.

Lucy knew the pain of having precious family items stolen. Her father had taken a gold necklace his mother had given her and pawned it one day, to put a bet on the horses. He'd sworn Lucy to secrecy over that loss. Lucy had witnessed her mum's pain on being unable to find her own mother's engagement ring, never confronting Lucy's father over taking it to pay off some debt. But they were mere trinkets when compared to a Stradivarius. The loss of an heirloom so precious would have hurt a family deeply.

Now her father was trying to take the violin too.

It was yet another reason she'd come to Lasserno after her life had imploded. The solicitor she was paying so much for had said her father would have a hard time proving the violin hadn't been properly gifted to Lucy. But if her mother couldn't get any mention of it struck out of the divorce proceedings, Lucy knew the true value of the instrument would be revealed. Her father's solicitors had already asked for a valuation.

She'd been assailed by twin dreads: losing her violin in a court battle and having it sold to some investor, or losing it to the family from whom it might have been taken over three-quarters of a century before.

She couldn't live with the suspicion that her violin might not have been given willingly, being stolen instead. Her father's lack of honesty had taught her the true importance of that moral quality. She'd never be like him. And this castle and Stefano Moretti might hold the truth that her Stradivarius hadn't been handed over as a generous symbol of thanks but was actually the spoils of war.

It wasn't hers to keep. It might never have been.

She didn't know what she'd do if that was the truth, because the most important parts of her professional career had been spent playing it. Losing her violin would be like losing part of herself. She may as well cut off her arm. Was it too much to ask that the person she might have to relinquish it to would be someone who deserved it? Who'd value it as she did?

The door opened and Stefano walked in, carrying a tray. Any dark thoughts were swept away by the glorious smell of something sweet and chocolatey filling the room. Her mouth watered. Stefano placed the tray on the table, and handed her a cup filled with thick, dark hot chocolate. He'd pushed back the sleeves of his sweater, exposing strong, muscular forearms. The pianist in her orchestra had forearms like that, from hours of practice. They'd never really appealed—or so she'd thought. This man's, though, with the tanned skin and all the dark hair… She could sit and contemplate their wonders for hours.

But illicit musings about her reluctant host weren't going to get her anywhere. The hot chocolate, however… She clutched the cup in her hands, letting it warm her. Took a hefty sip of its creamy sweetness. Eyed the delicious-looking plate of food—a small selection of meats, cheese, bread.

She sighed with happiness. 'Thank you.'

'Prego.' Stefano sat in an armchair beside the glowing fire. 'But I have some unfortunate news.'

He leaned back, one foot slung casually over his knee, a picture of masculinity. Nothing about him looked as if he was about to impart anything unfortunate. He appeared almost smug, with one eyebrow raised and the barest curve of his lips.

'I've called Bruno, who tells me the snow has set in and it won't be safe to retrieve your car…or you.'

Her heart raced—or that could just be all the sugar in her steaming drink. 'For how long?'

He shrugged. 'A few days. The roads are unpredictable when it snows. You'll have to stay here until they're passable. Black ice makes conditions treacherous.'

Stay in the castle. With the Count and no other people.

Tightness banded her chest, making it hard to breathe. She reached up and unzipped her puffer jacket a little, trying to get some air. 'I knew there were good reasons I hated winter.'

'I'm sorry. Bruno will have his snow plough out soon enough, but for now we're at the mercy of the weather.'

'It's not your fault,' she said. Though even in casual clothes the man in front of her looked so commanding that she was surprised he couldn't control the weather's whims with a flick of his hand. 'Back in Australia I thought snow sounded romantic, you know? All pristine, white and soft-looking. I couldn't wait to see it in real life, rather than in photographs.'

But the reality was all too different from her blissful fantasies of spending time in front of roaring fires, drinking hot chocolate, like she was now, and toasting marshmallows. The pervasive grey of it had sunk under her skin and sapped all happiness. Ever since the day she'd come home to their tiny Salzburg flat and found Viktor stoking the home fires with someone else. Even more humiliating, the woman was a viola player from the orchestra.

And if that wasn't the last nail in the coffin of her own personal *annus horribilis*, it was the fact that Viktor now sat in the lead violinist's chair instead of her. She had to wonder whether their relationship had meant anything to him at all. When she'd been pouring out her secret fears and insecurities to a man she believed she could trust, had he simply been mining them so he could undermine *her* and steal the concert leader's position she'd worked so hard for?

'I take it you weren't born somewhere cold?' Stefano said, pulling her back to the present with that smooth, deep voice. As sweet and tempting as the luscious drink in her mug.

'I'm a child of the subtropics. Snow's a disappointment. Cold and wet. Highly overrated.'

The corners of his lips tugged upwards the tiniest of fractions, but Lucy wouldn't call it a smile.

'What possessed a woman from Australia who hates winter to live somewhere it snows?'

She shrugged. 'Work.' It had been the opportunity of a lifetime. One that had now slipped through her cramped and injured hands. 'I'm a member of an orchestra. Principal violinist.'

Although it wasn't as if she could really play much right now, needing time to recover from the injury which had been quietly plaguing her. Fodder for the nasty rumours which now saw her here, on enforced leave to 'consider her future'.

Stefano cocked his head. In the gloomy afternoon light his eyes showed no colour, just intense dark focus, all fixed on her. 'I'm patron of Lasserno's Symphony Orchestra. You're young for such a huge responsibility.'

Something about those words sparked a simmering coal of anger inside her—one she'd been carrying for weeks. Since discovering that her violin might not be hers, since her father had tried to claim it in the divorce, since realising Viktor's treachery.

Viktor had given her guidance on her playing. She'd appreciated it in the beginning. He was older, brilliant in his own right, and she'd wanted to be perfect, always striving for more. He used to tell her that she hadn't lived enough, that because of her youth she'd lacked nuance. That if she didn't practise harder, and more, she'd fail.

Lucy had tried not to let his observations eat at her confidence and self-belief, but she recognised now that this was what he'd been trying to do. She wondered, in retrospect, whether their relationship had any truth to it, or whether he'd always had his eyes fixed on her principal violinist's role.

'At twenty-four, I'm not the youngest who's ever been principal violinist. And my position comes through hard work. Dedication. Determination. You're reported to have taken on the role of Prince Arcuri's private secretary when you were around my age. Was that too young for such a huge responsibility?'

His whole body stiffened. A look crossed his face and he almost flinched, as if in pain.

'All the members of my family commence service with the Crown when our monarch requests it. As for you… My words weren't meant as a criticism. I've no doubt of your determination, since you've walked here in this weather with your bags, one of which weighs enough to sink a boat. I assume that's your violin?'

He nodded to the case sitting next to her on the couch. She nodded too, and reached out to place her hand protectively on the travelling case.

'Yes, it's always with me.' She'd left her other violins, those she used for practice, stored with the orchestra. This one would remain by her side—especially now.

'I'd like to hear you play.'

Her heart jumped, pounding at her ribs. Once, she'd loved playing for anyone who asked. The joy of it…the way the music sang through her. Now it was as if the pain in her hands was a punishment—a sign of being *weak*. Her confidence in all things had been shattered.

She stretched her left hand again. It had suffered during the kilometres upon kilometres when she'd clutched the steering wheel in a strangling grip.

Lucy tried to ignore the stiffness plaguing her hand, reached out and grabbed some bread, cheese, meat. Made herself an open sandwich.

She wondered if she'd ever really play again. Whether she'd want to—whether the passion remained to make her strive for greatness and perfection when everything seemed so broken. Though in not playing, she was only half a person. Since the age of five, she'd rarely been without a violin in her hands. Lucy didn't know who she was without it.

'Maybe later,' she said. 'It's been a long drive.'

She couldn't admit her injury to him—not when she hoped to impress rather than disappoint the man who held the future of her violin in his hands. Her inability to play had left her bruised and vulnerable, as if an essential part of her had been lost.

But that was a thought for another day. The food was too tempting, and her stomach grumbled, so she took a welcome bite of her sandwich. She savoured the explosion of flavour in her mouth, the spice of the meat, the creamy saltiness of the cheese. She closed her eyes and almost moaned in delight at the combination.

'Ooh, this is *delicious*.'

All the while she had a prickling sensation at the back of her neck, as if she was being watched. She knew that Stefano was looking at her—that was normal, they were in the room together. This was something more. As if she was being studied. Not that it was an unpleasant sensation—rather a blistering awareness of something *more*. Like being drizzled with syrup and…licked.

The shock of that thought zapped through her like an electric current.

Lucy opened her eyes and Stefano leaned forward, forearms on his knees, hands clasped in front of him, long fingers, perfect nails. Firelight flickered in the depths of his dark eyes. There was the merest of frowns on his face. She pressed back into the couch, her heart kicking up its thready rhythm again. It should scare her, but she wasn't sure fear was what her rapid heartbeat was trying to tell her.

She couldn't sit there any longer without saying something. 'What? Have I got food on my chin?'

It was as if the words shook him out of a kind of trance. He leapt from his seat, and she was forced to look up at his imposing frame.

'Forgive me. I'm being a poor host. It's been too long since anyone's stayed here. You've had a harrowing day and must be exhausted.'

'Thank you. That's—'

'I'm sure you'd like to use the facilities and rest. I'll prepare your room.'

Then he stalked out through the door, and she once again watched him go. Wondering what on earth she'd done wrong.

CHAPTER THREE

STEFANO KNEW HOW to be a gracious host. He'd held countless parties and soirees, allowing him to navigate polite society, and had once been able to slip into the role as if it was another of his bespoke suits. Yet nothing about him felt gracious or polite tonight.

He sat at the vast table in his ancestral home's dining room. A place where he'd not eaten for years, preferring the castle kitchen or his suite for his meals. The memories here were of lonely dinners, where children had most definitely been seen and not heard—decorative items to be brought out and cooed over, once bathed and polished, then kissed on the forehead and tucked into bed.

His parents had often left them to the nanny and taken themselves to the capital, where they'd stay for weeks. Only occasional phone calls to check on his schooling had reminded him that he had parents at all. Court intrigue and maintaining their position in society had been their preferred and natural environment. Children were a necessity to maintain the family line, and so long as they appeared to be following their lessons and behaving it was enough.

He had never been viewed as an individual by them, but as a means to ensure his family's power. His father had been a remote and imposing figure, whose lessons had been all about duty and not disgracing the family name. And his mother's last words to him, when rumours of Stefano's fall had reached her ears, had told him all he needed to know about where her thoughts lay.

'It's a blessing your father isn't alive to see you now.'

But those weren't the thoughts driving his dark mood tonight. He'd sat in his study after taking Lucy to her room. Engaged his investigator to cease his efforts in chasing a ghost and turn his attentions instead to Lucy and her family. Then he'd heard it, drifting through the lonely castle halls. The sweet sound of a violin. Not a tune, as such, but the heavenly swell of a few perfect notes.

He'd forgotten how much he missed music, here in his mountain exile. His patronage of Lasserno's orchestra had never been an obligation for him, but a true labour of love—much to Celine's disdain, because she didn't enjoy classical music.

Rather than concentrating on his task of retrieving the Crown Jewels, he'd spent too many hours straining to hear more of the pure, single notes Lucy played. He'd researched her achievements. She had strings of awards and accomplishments. And then there were the videos… No sight of the windblown waif who'd arrived unannounced and unwelcome on his threshold, but a glimpse of perfection, with polished skin and smoothed strawberry gold hair. Lucy played like a celestial being. With her face a study of emotional pain mixed with joy, she looked like an angel about to fall.

Stefano craved to be the man who caught her.

But he had no right to these fruitless desires. Now the woman herself sat to his left, about a quarter of the way down the table. As far away as he could politely put her without having to shout when engaging in conversation.

He'd managed, for her sake, to coax the castle's groaning heating system into warming this room, so she'd shed her puffy blue monstrosity of a coat. A blessing and a curse. Because underneath it she wore a dress. Long-sleeved, black, with no embellishments. It should have looked plain and unremarkable, but the simple fabric and cut transfixed him as if the cloth had been woven by magic. The way it wrapped round her slender body... Tied at the waist with a draped skirt swishing at her knees allowing glimpses of the elegant sweep of her calves...

He took a sip of the wine which he'd grabbed from the palace cellar earlier. It hadn't been so long that he'd forgotten how to act around a beautiful woman, but she interested him far too much. It was as if he was a teenage boy again, hoping to catch the alluring swell of a woman's calf, the tempting curve of her breast.

He'd known the moment he'd opened the door to her that she was a distraction, and he'd been right. She may be the answer to one of his country's oldest questions, but Stefano didn't have time to be diverted from his task by errant desire. His siblings were counting on him and he had the terrible sense that time was running out—like watching the last grains of sand trickling through an hourglass.

'This meal's delicious.'

Lucy carefully placed down her fork and looked at him, head cocked a little to the side. Her eyes were wide, golden light gleaming in them from the chandeliers glittering above the table. He should have lit candles. She'd look beautiful in the soft, flickering light, like she had in the glow from the fireplace this afternoon... But this was not that kind of meal, filled with romance and seduction. It was all about fact-finding rather than fanciful thoughts about bathing her in the perfect light.

'You made it yourself?'

'*Si*. The family chef taught me a few things when I was younger. Said I should learn to feed myself. Also to "impress the ladies". I believe that was his most important consideration for any young man.'

Except Celine had never been enthused by his efforts. She'd always wanted to dine at the finest restaurants in Lasserno, even when he'd had enough of them and craved a home-cooked meal. Lucy, on the other hand...

He'd spent a tortured half-hour watching her devour the simple pasta dish he'd made. He'd make pasta for the woman every night she was here just to witness her pleasure as she ate it. To watch her tongue dart out almost guiltily, licking some stray sauce from the glorious pout of her lower lip.

'I'm sure you made a huge impression.'

She must have noticed him staring. It seemed to be a strange affliction plaguing him.

She tucked her hair behind her ears, the tips of which were tinted with a faint flush of pink. 'You've impressed me.'

'It was my pleasure.'

Her words shouldn't have moved him, but it was as if an ember had been lit deep inside. A lazy kind of heat slid through him at her enjoyment of the meal he'd made. He couldn't allow it to continue. She was simply another part of the job he must focus upon. Nothing more.

'However, there was no need to dress for dinner.' Her warm winter clothes were much better, with their many layers which hid her from his unruly gaze.

Lucy shrugged, blissfully unaware of his inner struggle. 'I wasn't sure. When you dropped me at my room you did announce, "Dinner is at nine in the dining room. I will escort you there." I've never had dinner in a castle with a count before. It sounded pretty formal.'

She appeared earnest enough. However, the corners of her mouth might have twitched…or perhaps that was his fertile imagination. She seemed to invoke it.

'As you can see…' he held his arms out, motioning to his jeans, his sweater '…no formality here.'

She fixed him with her honeyed gaze and it was as if he were skewered to the spot, like an insect under a pin. It seemed his words were all the invitation she'd needed, because she was really studying him. Her eyes were on his face, sliding down to his chest, along his arms… Something about the appraisal was as intimate as it was overt. Then she looked away and the release was like a snap, sharp and brutal. He wanted her heated gaze on him again. It seemed as vital as his next breath.

'I'll remember that for next time,' she said. 'If there is a next time. The snow might clear by tomorrow and then Bruno can collect me.'

Not if the weather reports were anything to go by.

And even if the snow cleared, she was a woman who might solve the mystery that would pave the way to a kind of forgiveness of his family by his best friend. But most of all he might finally be able to forgive himself. He just needed to remember how to charm. To convince her to stay when it was clear she wished to be anywhere else.

He had been charming once; it was a particular skill required of his job. When the Prince had been required to make harsh decisions, Stefano's role had called upon him to smooth out the sharp edges. Craft messages to soothe and placate.

He needed someone to smooth out his own edges now. All of him felt sharp enough to draw blood. The past few months had been about coercing the reluctant aristocracy into returning gems that weren't theirs. Polite conversation had no place in those efforts. He'd left polite society well behind.

'The weather's set in. But even if it hadn't, you're welcome to stay here rather than in the village.'

She finished another mouthful of pasta. Took a delicate sip of her own wine. Her glass was mostly full whereas his third glass was almost empty.

'That's kind of you, but I've paid for a room in the *pensione*. Plus, it's warmer than here.'

'*Mi dispiace.* I'm afraid my hospitality in that regard is lacking.'

'Well, the room you gave me is lovely. I've never stayed anywhere with frescoes on the ceiling. The frolicking cherubs are sweet.'

'It was a nursery once, and then the nanny's room, which is why it's...sweet. The ceilings of some of the other rooms here serve to remind humanity of all its failings.'

Those were the rooms he now avoided, with their pictures of final judgement and hellscapes. It was as if the building itself judged him, and Stefano didn't need the stones and mortar here reminding him of how far he'd fallen. Anyhow, he didn't want to talk about the castle's many Renaissance wonders—although he could, for hours. He had more pressing things on his agenda.

'What are you hoping to achieve in Varno? Your letter says your grandfather spoke of it and you mentioned your family history?'

He'd found her letter in his desk, bundled unceremoniously with other correspondence he didn't have the stomach for. Most of what was in it she'd already told him—about her grandfather being shot down over Italy and that he'd recently passed away. Meaning she was all he had to solve this old mystery. But they were tantalising hints rather than anything explicit. The letter had been a polite request for a meeting. She'd made the trip sound almost like a kind of pilgrimage.

'You found my letter? At least something's gone right.'

Those words held a worn and tired quality to them. As if a lot had not gone right for her lately. Something niggled at him—a desire to ask why—but he had more important answers to seek, and her problems weren't his to solve.

'I'm sorry for your loss.' Whatever his thoughts on what her grandfather might have done, he had some humanity left. It was the tiniest shred, but for this mo-

ment he grasped it. 'You said he passed away recently?
He must have been a great age.'

'He was. Ninety-nine. He lived a long and full life,
but it's never easy to lose someone you love.'

Lucy toyed with a stray piece of spaghetti on her
plate, chasing it around with her fork. He allowed the
silence to stretch uncomfortably. He found people often
preferred filling it rather than saying nothing.

Lucy gave up her pursuit of the rogue pasta and set
her cutlery down. She took a deep breath. Sighed. 'My
grandfather used to tell me stories about the great kindness of the people here—especially in the Varno province. I wanted to see for myself. Research my family
history a bit. Maybe visit the places he did... see if the
people were as kind and generous as he said.'

Desperate and gullible was a better description, for
his family at least. With the enemy threatening, they'd
hoped a man they'd thought honourable, with allied
links to the underground movement, could save the one
precious national heirloom they hadn't been able to hide
in time. Still, Stefano had never understood why his
great-grandfather, Lasserno's Crown Jeweller, had taken
the rash action of trusting a random stranger.

'Aren't people in Salzburg friendly?' he asked.

'I made what I thought was a good life there.'

He well understood how what you believed your life
to be and what it really was could turn out to be vastly
different, though she didn't elaborate. Everything about
her seemed distant, cautious... But personal information such as this, whilst intriguing, was not what he
sought from her.

'Did your grandfather talk much of the war?'

'No. It damaged him. I think he felt guilt, mainly, for those he'd lost…or couldn't save.'

Nothing about a ring. That would be too easy.

'My great-aunt was only a young woman when she died in the war. My family never spoke of it,' Stefano said. 'Lasserno suffered during its occupation. Sometimes recollections can be too painful.'

'All I know is that my grandfather always remembered the people here. It seemed that he loved the place and had left a little piece of his heart behind from the way he talked about it. In his last weeks he mentioned someone. A woman.'

'Not your grandmother?'

Lucy shook her head. 'Much to my mother's surprise. But in the end his memory was all over the place. He was pretty confused. Anyhow…when he talked about Lasserno he always told me if I loved something, or *someone*, to fight for it. Hold it close because life was short.' She gave a huff of a laugh. Her jaw clenched hard, she stared straight ahead, her eyes distant.

'You don't agree?'

'It sounds romantic, but it only works if a person wants to stay. How do you know if someone loves you as much as you think you love them, or loves you in the same way?'

She turned to him, her eyes tight, as if she was recalling fresh pain. He had nothing for her. Stefano had believed he and Celine would be married by now, yet all she'd wanted was his family name. The title and the position, not the man. More fool him. All she'd proved was that love was for the gullible.

There was no turning back now. His naivety was

lost. And he couldn't forget her parting words—was now asking the same question of himself, almost daily. Who was he if he was not working for the Prince? Because that was all he'd been in the end: Alessio's private secretary. Yet he found he wanted to try and give Lucy an answer—one that wasn't steeped in bitterness.

'You can never know. You can only guess or hope.'

She smoothed the fabric of her dress. 'That might be fine for some people, but it leaves the door open to a world of pain. Is that good enough for you?'

Pain was his constant companion now. He didn't want to add more. All he craved was certainty. Not this sensation of life constantly shifting underneath him.

'I'm not much for guessing or hoping.'

She raised her glass in a mocking kind of toast. 'Here's to us.'

With that hard glint in her eye he expected her to down the rest of the glass. Instead, she took a tiny sip. He decided to make up for her reticence. Even though his thoughtless mouthful was a crime committed against the magnificent wine.

'Why are you a cynic, Lucy?' He shouldn't care, but it was a question he genuinely wanted the answer to. What memories made her stare into the distance, with her mouth tight and her eyes strained?

'Life in the orchestra taught me a few lessons about hard work and paying high prices,' she said, torturing the napkin on her lap.

'It must require a great deal of practice.'

'Three to four hours of personal practice a day, leaving aside rehearsals. Or that's how much I liked to do.

Some people want or demand more. In the end, I found that…counterproductive.'

'If you need to practice here, you're welcome. We have a music room.'

Lucy's eyes lit up. Such a simple suggestion had made her happy again. Her brightness warmed him. For a moment he never wanted that glow of hers to fade.

'I'd love to see it…even though I'm taking a bit of a break from performing.'

She flexed the slender fingers of her left hand, then pressed her right thumb deep into her palm and rubbed. She bit hard into her lower lip and the troubled look was back again.

'You're free to explore the castle if you wish.'

'Really? Is there anywhere I can't go?'

Strangely, he found he didn't mind where she went. His suggestion appeared to please her. A gentle smile teased her lips and he wanted to keep that look on her face.

'Most of the formal rooms are unused, but you can open any door…look at whatever you want.'

'What if I get lost?'

'You can call me.' He slipped his phone from his pocket. 'What's your number?'

Lucy gave it to him and he sent her a text. Something in her vicinity buzzed with an alert.

'This is exciting. You said you don't allow tourists here?'

'Never. But you've told me you aren't a tourist, so the ghosts of my ancestors shouldn't punish me.' Not for this sin at least. There were many more to haunt him over.

'I'll let you in on a secret,' she said, lowering her voice and leaning forward in her seat. 'I bet I fit the dictionary definition of one.'

He leaned forward too. In these moments the sensation curling inside him was strange and unfamiliar. Like happiness. Around her, he couldn't help himself.

Lucy's eyes widened a fraction. He lowered his voice. 'I won't tell anyone if you don't.'

In response Lucy laughed, and the sound rippled through him with a wave of pleasure so intense he thought he could spend all of his time making her smile.

That was his reminder. As she laughed in her seat, glowing with what appeared to be true joy, he knew he needed to remember the job he must do.

'So, Tourist Lucy, how long do you have in Lasserno?'

He should find out how much time he'd have to try and extract the information he sought—because he needed subtlety. Especially if her family's fortunes had been made on the back of that coronation ring. What would his investigators find? Wealth? A sudden change of circumstance?

But now, as he watched Lucy, it was as if a light's dimmer switch had been turned down. Everything in her faded. He regretted dimming her glow, because he was sure his words were the cause.

'A few weeks…maybe a month. I have things I need to do in Salzburg. Moving apartments.'

'Your orchestra must be missing you. You have an impressive biography.'

She dug her thumb into the palm of her left hand again, rubbing hard.

'The second violin will slot into my role nicely.' Her voice was sharp and discordant. She grabbed the napkin from her lap, placed it on the table. 'Do you mind? I'm very tired and I think I need to go to sleep.'

Lucy stood, so he stood. How could he tell her he didn't want her to go? Or, even better, tell her that she should invite him to go to bed with her? Keep her warm…

'Please…' Lucy looked at him, her eyes glittering like the chandeliers above them. Were they tears? Before he could say anything, she grabbed her coat. 'I can find my own way to my room. The dinner was beautiful. Thank you again.'

And as she rushed out through the door and left him standing at his seat, it was as if all the lights in the room had finally been snuffed out.

CHAPTER FOUR

LUCY SHOULD BE EXHAUSTED. However, every time she tried to close her eyes her thoughts shifted randomly, like autumn leaves tossed by the wind.

There was no point to them. Ruminating about what had happened couldn't change the reality of her life being a mess. But Stefano…his questions. They'd been the sorts of things any person might ask her in general conversation, but it had become all too much. She'd run before she'd collapsed, weeping into her empty plate.

She rolled over in bed to face the fire, which had died down to cherry embers. The part of the sheet she was not immediately lying on chilled against her body and she shivered. Even with warm socks on her feet, she seemed numb. It was as if she'd be cold for ever.

Although tonight at dinner, the way Stefano had looked at her… His eyes, so dark, had pierced right through her. There'd been a hectic glitter in them when she'd removed her coat and he'd taken in her figure-hugging black dress. The one she'd hastily thrown it into her suitcase when she'd fled her apartment after Viktor's betrayal. *That* look had heated her to her core.

Lucy wasn't sure why she'd put on the dress for dinner tonight. She'd hoped to wear it for their first meeting, had her trip gone to plan. Maybe it's because it was something she'd performed in, and had made her feel competent when nothing about her life over the past months had given her any sense that she knew what she was doing.

Anyhow, what was life if not a performance of some kind? It had seemed for months that she was an actor in her own life, rather than really taking charge. Coming to Lasserno was meant to be her first step in doing that and here she was, trapped in a freezing castle. Shivering, she threw back the cloud-soft down duvet and hopped out of bed, hurrying across the thick carpet to her coat. She shrugged it over her pyjamas, found a pair of fingerless gloves and slid them on before grabbing the duvet, picking up her violin case and huddling in front of the pretty little marble fireplace.

Whilst she was already cracked and broken, her violin wasn't, and she knew the dangers of low humidity and too much cold on the precious old wood. Sitting there, Lucy tried to ignore the pervasive little voice that whispered she was a fraud, even given her position in the orchestra. All those extra hours she'd practised at Viktor's instigation... He'd convinced her he was making her do it out of love, when all it had given her was the beginnings of an over-use injury and a niggling belief that somehow that injury was *her* fault—evidence of an inherent weakness.

What she needed was a cheery big fire...more light to chase away the shadows. Just...*more*. The sitting room had been much warmer, brighter. Maybe she'd find that room, since there was no way she'd ever sleep here—not now. She supposed she could text Stefano to ask for extra blankets, but it was late and she didn't want to wake him…

Her indecision curdled in her stomach, the sensation working its way up, grabbing her round the throat. It was almost like the nerves before a solo performance—but that was a thrilling kind of sensation that overwhelmed most of the fear. There was nothing thrilling about the way she felt now, with this paralysis stealing over her.

'It's not in the stars to hold our destiny, Lucy, but in ourselves.'

That's what her grandfather had always said, as they'd sat together on warm sunny days on the patio of his old home. He'd make a cup of tea and give her biscuits and talk.

She shut her eyes, fought back tears at his loss. He might have been an old man, but he'd been a quiet place of stability compared to the chaos of her father. She knew what he'd been trying to tell her—that she had to make her own way rather than dream about it.

Right now, her destiny involved somewhere warmer for her and her instrument. She stood with her violin case, still clutching the duvet round her, then left her room and padded through the generously carpeted halls filled with gilt-framed artwork and antiques, but happily absent any judgemental family portraits, until she reached a familiar door with an orange glow flickering underneath.

Lucy grabbed the icy handle, opening the door to an empty room. A low lamp still shone, and the fire in the large marble fireplace burned brightly, with a more generous heat than the one in her bedroom. She put down her violin and grabbed some cushions from the couch, dropping them to the floor. Wrapping herself and her violin case in the duvet, she was soon lying down in front of the fire, trying not to think of anything but how warm and comfortable it was on the makeshift bed she'd made.

She watched the flickering flames. And finally her eyelids became heavy and her thoughts drifted…

'What's this? Why are you on the floor?'

Lucy jumped and sat up, the duvet falling from her shoulders. Everything was fuzzy, as if her head had been stuffed with cotton wool. She rubbed her grainy eyes and looked at a clock on the mantelpiece. It was well past midnight.

'I'm trying to sleep.'

Stefano was halfway into the room, holding the neck of a bottle and a short glass, still dressed as he'd been for dinner. He looked effortlessly casual and handsome in a way that almost hurt for a mere mortal like her. His hair, gleaming black and tousled. His jaw grazed by a fashionable stubble.

He glared at the bed she'd made for herself as if she'd committed some personal offence against his furniture. Which she likely had, since she'd disassembled his couch.

'This isn't sleeping. This is nesting like a *topino*. A little mouse.'

'I'm not a mouse.'

Viktor had accused her playing of being timid. It was why she'd practised more…harder. Trying to inject some of the elusive passion he'd claimed was lacking into it. She flexed her fingers, but there was no stiffness or numbness right now. She took it as a small win in months of none.

'I couldn't sleep in the bedroom, so I thought I'd come here.'

Stefano toed the door closed and sank into an armchair. Uncapping the bottle, he poured a generous load of clear fluid into his glass and took a mouthful, rather than a sip. He'd consumed most of the bottle of wine at dinner like that.

She wrapped the duvet tight round her shoulders. 'What are you doing up so late?'

'Working.' He took another hefty swig from his glass and stared into the fire.

'Sounds like you need another job. What's so important that you have to work after midnight?'

'A special project.'

His eyes glittered like obsidian in the golden light of the room, boring into her. She shifted under the intense appraisal. Everything about him seemed to still, like a predator watching its prey.

'I'm trying to find some of the country's lost treasures.'

She swallowed past the sick knot in her throat and placed a hand on the violin case under the blankets, drawing it closer towards her. She could mention the Stradivarius now—it was almost the perfect opening. Except she didn't know the man, or how he'd react...

'What kind of treasures?' Lucy held her breath, waiting for his answer.

His hand gripped the arm of the chair, his fingers denting the fabric. 'Some gems from the royal collection.'

Her shoulders dropped. Jewels—not a lost Stradivarius. 'I'd have thought you'd go to the police about that.'

He dragged his hand over his face and she realised that once she got past how supernaturally handsome he was, Stefano also looked tired. Underneath his eyes his skin had a slightly greyish quality, in contrast to the healthy bronze elsewhere.

'Some responsibilities are mine alone,' he said.

Those words sounded as if they carried the expectations of a nation. He gazed into some unseen distance, as though imagining a future that might be there.

'How's your search been going?'

His focus returned to her and she didn't like it. It was a strange kind of appraisal, as though he was cataloguing her worth. She was well aware of how she must look, her hair likely a bird's nest, wearing her coat and her pyjamas. A mess—kind of like her unravelling life.

'I'm hoping for an unexpected improvement,' he said.

There was something about him that seemed so bleak as he downed the remaining drink in his glass. He uncapped the bottle, poured another shot, seemingly intent on drowning unspoken sorrows. Her heartbeat bounded, sickening and thready in the ominous silence that descended between them.

She wrapped her arms round her knees. 'What are you drinking?'

'Bruno's version of grappa.' He held up the glass of clear, gleaming liquid. 'Do you want some?'

'Is it strong?'

He snorted, his expression brooding and dark. 'It can help a person forget all manner of sins.'

'What sins do you have to forget?'

The corner of his mouth kicked up in the barest of smiles, but there was nothing happy about the way he looked in this moment. 'Too many to count,' he said, taking another hefty sip.

Her stomach turned over in uncomfortable knots, the way it always had when her mum was away, performing, and she had to stay alone with her father. He'd used to like a drink with dinner. Then it had turned into drinks after dinner, then with lunch, and then in the mornings before breakfast...

'Could you...not?' Her voice came out in a whisper, as those memories crept back through the cracks in her consciousness. Memories of staying in her bedroom whilst her dad ranted about needing to 'babysit'. As if he wasn't her father, who should be happy to look after his only child.

'Not what?'

'Drink so much.'

'I have no problem here.' He looked at the glass cradled almost negligently in his long and perfect fingers, then back at her, raising his eyebrow. 'Are you judging me, Lucy? Because if you are, I suggest that you...how do you say it? Take a number.'

There was something simmering underneath here, like magma boiling in the rocks below. You might not be able to see it, but it roiled away nonetheless, waiting to burst through a fissure when you least expected.

'I'm a woman alone in your house and you look like you want to get very drunk.'

She chewed on her bottom lip, almost wishing she'd said nothing. But surely he could see why the situation might worry her? Of course, he'd probably never been worried by anything in his life…

He hesitated, then put the glass down on a side table and cocked his head, his eyes narrowing. 'You've had experience of this.'

She shrugged.

'Who had the problem? Did they ever hurt you?'

Stefano's voice was low and cool. It might have been soothing in a way, but it carried a steel edge that suggested he wanted to take on the role of avenging angel on her behalf. His cold certainty melted away her apprehension, replacing it with something softer, warmer. These conflicting feelings made no sense. Still, nothing much in her life did right now.

'My father liked to drink. He never touched me, but…'

All those times he'd blamed someone else for his failures. Business ventures going wrong. Bets lost. As a child, she hadn't understood it. As an adult, she'd come to learn that her father had trouble taking any responsibility for his actions or his life. He expected everything to be handed to him. Even her violin.

Your mother never really gave it to you. She only pretended it was yours to hide it from me. I won't let her get away with it…

The implication was clear. His alcoholism. His anger. It wasn't his fault. It was her mother's. Hers.

'Words and actions can hurt more than fists,' Stefano said, in a way that sounded far too knowing.

She wondered what could possibly have hurt *him*.

He had everything. A title, power, a castle… There was a veneer of perfection about him that seemed hard to crack, although she'd glimpsed a few things. The apparent tiredness. Those moments when his gaze became unfocussed and distant.

'My father's a complicated man. He's an only child and was doted on by his parents. They gave him everything—he just couldn't seem to hang on to it. He likes drowning his sins too.'

Stefano pushed the bottle away from him with two long, elegant fingers. The look on his face was earnest and sure. 'Whilst you're in my home, this won't happen again.'

Something inside her let go, relaxed the tiniest of fractions, and the exhaustion that had threatened all day began to wash over her again.

'You're safe here, Lucy. You have nothing to fear from me.'

After months of not knowing who or what to believe, for a few moments of relief she allowed herself to accept Stefano's words to be true.

Stefano was certain that if he looked in a mirror he wouldn't like his reflection much right now. He'd made Lucy worried, perhaps afraid. Her eyes had been wide, her body tense. What sort of person *did* that? No one good, he was sure.

Having this woman think less of him didn't sit well. Huddled in front of the fire, beautiful and unkempt in the warm light of the room, she looked as if she needed a protector. Once, he'd have been that person. Caring, taking care. Now, he shouldn't be entrusted with anything precious because he'd destroy it. Still, he loathed it that Lucy might believe she needed protection from him.

'You can't sleep here on the floor.'

She curled her arms round herself, fingers gripping the edges of the duvet. 'It's okay. Really.' She grappled with something beside her—something angular.

Stefano frowned. 'What do you have under there with you?'

She shrugged. 'My violin.'

'Your *what*?'

Of all the answers, that was not one he'd expected her to give.

'I'm not the first violinist who's slept with one and I won't be the last.

'Why?'

'It's a three-hundred-year-old instrument, and if it gets too cold and dry the wood might crack.'

It dawned on him now why she was here, in this room with the large fireplace. He felt the sickening sensation of one more layer of guilt joining the rest.

'You're cold. I'm freezing you. Lucy, you should have called me. I'd have found you more blankets.'

'I thought you'd be asleep. Anyhow, I don't think more blankets will work. It's the bedroom. The fireplace is tiny and the fire went out. Don't worry about me—here's comfortable.'

He was the devil who'd done this to her, and he'd make it right. 'Take my room. It has a larger fireplace.'

'I—I couldn't. Where will you go?'

He looked at the long couch where he'd spent many nights sleeping. In his bedroom suite, where every

Count of Varno had slept, he was suffocated by the weight of his history. How he'd destroyed it all. That was why he'd taken to this room, with a blanket, a fire and a bottle of alcohol to drown out the self-recrimination.

'I rarely sleep more than a few hours at a time. Please let me show you, then you can decide.'

He stood as Lucy clambered up from the floor in her coat. Then he noticed her feet. 'Are they…socks with unicorn cats?'

Her cheeks flushed a soft pink. She blew out a huff of breath. 'You're really not seeing me at my finest. I'd planned an official visit, where I looked more…competent than this. I promise I know how to be an adult when I try.'

'My sister's studying teaching. I'm sure she has a pair of socks with cats on them. Not unicorn cats… She would be envious.'

'Don't forget, these are *rainbow* unicorn cats. It's all about the rainbows. My gloves match, too.'

She held out one hand and wiggled her fingers.

'It is a fashion statement I'll never forget. Perhaps I'll try to find some for my sister, as a gift.'

She smiled, and it hit him in the solar plexus like a punch. All the breath left him. That smile brimmed with an innocent-looking joy, no artifice. It lit up the room, taking a grey world and turning it multi-coloured and gleaming, like the rainbows adorning her hands and feet.

'You're a good brother. I can give you the website. I promise she'll love you for it.'

He stilled. If only Lucy knew, she wouldn't be saying these things. His actions had successfully torpe-

doed his siblings' future. He must never forget this was
the woman who might have information that could recover everything for him. That wouldn't happen if she
didn't trust him and wasn't prepared to talk—which
meant he had to find the shred of humanity he'd buried deep inside.

He was sure she knew something. He'd seen the
tightening around her eyes when he'd said he was
searching for the nation's lost treasures at dinner. She
hid things—he just wasn't sure what.

'Let me take your violin.'

She hesitated before relinquishing it.

As he took the handle of the case their fingers
brushed and it was as if time slowed, the stroke of skin
over skin seeming to take minutes rather than the briefest of seconds. Lucy made a sound, an exhalation. The
shimmering heat of that touch flowed through him.
His heart pumped hard and fast. She looked up at him,
eyes wide, as if she'd seen him for the first time. Her
lips parted.

They stood close, a world of clothes between them,
and yet it was as if he was completely exposed. A small
sprinkle of freckles dotted her nose, and Stefano wanted
to take his time, count each one. He wondered if there
were more on areas exposed to the sunlight when the
weather was warm, on her shoulders, her chest…

He stopped, shook himself from the fantasy. 'Follow
me.' He cleared his throat, his voice rough and raw. 'We
need to get you warm.'

That devil's voice in his head began hinting at the
many enjoyable ways he could keep this beautiful

woman warm and occupied for days. Ways which would allow him to forget the weight of obligation, his failures.

But he didn't deserve that kind of relief. Not the pleasure, not the softness. If she knew anything at all about him she wouldn't be looking at him now with a kind of naked wonder written all over her face.

He began to walk and she followed, still wrapped in the down duvet which trailed behind her like an oversized cape. She appeared regal, almost as if she owned the space, making him feel like an impostor.

'This place is amazing,' she said. 'More like a museum than a family home.'

In many ways she was right, but still, this place *had* been a home to him as much as a showcase. He'd tried to make it so for his brother and sister, when his parents had left them here to pursue their own ambitions, and before those ambitions had become his too, since he really had nothing else.

'The benefits of a five-hundred-year-old family history,' he said.

'I can't imagine the…the responsibility of all that behind you. What that would be like to have always sitting on your shoulders. Or are you so used to it that it doesn't matter?'

It was all he knew. The responsibility simply *existed*. There were expectations he'd accepted because there was no option or choice. It hadn't bothered him in the beginning—especially when the power of that obligation to something larger than himself had become like a drug. When he'd realised as he'd left his childhood and moved through his teens that sitting in the top echelons of his country's society was a good place to be.

That sickened him now, because in his arrogance he hadn't realised the privilege of his position and how easy it was to fall from the lofty pedestal his family had built for themselves.

'I simply…am.'

What more could he say? He was the Count of Varno. The Shield of the Crown. A role he'd never made the most of. He'd worn it like a cloak rather than wielded its power for anything worthwhile. Now the opportunity to do so was lost to him. The sting of self-recrimination was a constant reminder of how he'd failed. He didn't know how to be anything or anyone else.

'Do you ever wish the expectations had never existed? That you weren't who you were born to be?'

They'd reached the door of his room—a blessed relief, because she asked questions it was hard for him to answer, referred to things he couldn't think about lest he dwelled too hard on what he'd thrown away. But to the last question there was only one response he could give.

'Who am I if I'm not working for the Prince?'

Lucy's heart thumped an unsteady tempo, like some kind of wicked drumbeat. He was only being kind, putting her in his room where he hoped it would be warmer than in the chill that had settled over this whole place. More than the troublesome heating, it was an oppression, hanging like a grey pall over the castle. She couldn't shake the conviction that it was coming from the man who had now stopped walking in front of her in long, easy strides. There was a sense of brooding about him…something unfulfilled. She couldn't put her finger on it.

They'd reached a grand door—or at least grander than the other magnificent doors here—with an impressive coat of arms carved into the wood. Stefano stood next to her, a respectful distance away, holding her violin case. It made her prickly, nervous that his hands were on it when the only person who ever touched it now was her. Still, since he might be the true owner of the instrument, she thought she'd try it out for size. It didn't fit.

'You have a unicorn on your door,' she said. It was a fierce-looking unicorn, almost terrifying as it reared against a shield of some sort.

'It's a unicorn rampant.'

'Well, it does look a bit wild, with those eyes and its tongue.'

She turned to look at him and the corner of his mouth hitched. Her breath caught in anticipation, but she still couldn't call the move a smile.

'It's a heraldic term,' he said. 'Since the unicorn's rearing up. But you mustn't forget the dragon.'

How could she miss it? Rearing up as well, looking no less fierce than the unicorn.

'The dragon *rampant*, you mean? Not exactly a restful entrance to your bedroom. I suppose they have some suitably impressive meaning?'

He shrugged. 'Lasserno's herald could tell you more, but a unicorn represents courage, strength and virtue. The dragon is a defender...valiant.'

'A valiant defender with courage, strength and virtue? That's a lot to live up to.'

Stefano stared at his family crest, again appearing as though he was looking through it into a memory. Given the grim line of his mouth and the clench of his jaw, it wasn't a happy one.

'So I'm perpetually reminded,' he said.

This whole place appeared to haunt him. She felt an ache start inside, a sensation of empathy, because at least she'd been able to flee her apartment and her life for a while. Where was his escape, if not here?

'As impressive as it is, your family crest is sadly absent of rainbow unicorn cats.' She wiggled her sock-covered toes and looked up at him. That garnered another of his almost-smiles, and a snort which didn't sound at all dignified or aristocratic.

'After centuries of living with these honourable creatures I can see my family coat of arms is lacking. What do the unicorn cats represent?'

'Hmmm… Happiness, I guess? Which I suppose isn't very impressive.'

'It's an important quality, since so many fail to find it.' His head dropped, and his shoulders slumped in the smallest of ways which told a larger story. 'And I'm certain *you* would be much happier in a warm room and asleep after your long and arduous day.'

Stefano opened his bedroom door, flicked on a light and strode inside. She followed. Whilst what she'd seen of the rest of the castle had been designed to impress, this room was something else. Wine-red carpet as thick and soft as unmown grass. A massive marble fireplace, unlike the tiny elegant one in her room. A lounge suite in front of the fireplace that looked as if you'd sink into it and never want to leave. Walls lined in a deep, rich burgundy silk.

It was bold…sumptuous. Yet as impressive as the

whole space appeared, it was nothing compared to the centrepiece of the room. A four-poster bed that didn't look as if it had been built for any mere mortal, with its gleaming polished wood and a rich embroidered canopy in jewel tones completed the opulence of the room.

Stefano placed her violin case gently down in a corner, then moved to the fireplace, working on the fire. All the while she stood silent, just inside the doorway. The breath was tight in her chest. She couldn't sleep here. It was as if by being in this room she'd become immersed in him. It was far too close, too intimate. Like she would sink into him, be pulled under and drown.

'Come in and close the door,' he said, drawing her out of her heated imaginings.

Except watching him poking about in the fire, coaxing it to catch and burn with his sleeves pushed up, looking all manly and competent, just dragged her further into a kind of spell.

He stood and glared at the flames as if daring them to go out, his hands on his narrow hips, the whole move accentuating his broad shoulders backlit by the fire in the hearth. It was a masculine silhouette, but she didn't know why the picture it painted caused all of her to flood with a roaring heat. Really, she didn't need a fire in the room to keep her warm. All she needed was Stefano to stand around and...*brood*.

After a few moments, seemingly satisfied that the fire wasn't about to disobey him, he turned back to her, still stuck in the doorway. Frozen. He frowned. 'If you come inside and shut the door it'll keep the heat in.'

He'd obviously misunderstood her reticence. She probably looked like the frightened little mouse he'd accused her of being, and she refused to be that. Lucy stepped inside and shut the door behind her—then almost backed up against it. Because now he *stared*, as if she was some kind of fool. His intense black gaze was fixed on her. It should have been cold, that fathomless colour, but it reminded her of febrile summer nights in the subtropics back home.

She needed to say something which made sense. 'I *can't* sleep here in your room.'

The words spilled out in a voice that was a little too soft and a lot too breathy and left her exposed—as if she'd stripped off her clothes and was dancing about the room shamelessly naked. And that thought led inevitably to thoughts of him naked too…except he wouldn't be shameless. He would be glorious. Perfect, if the shape of him hinted at under his clothes was anything to go by. Or perhaps not hinted at but shouted out—loudly. With a megaphone.

Her cheeks burned. She wanted to clap her hands to them, to hide what was no doubt a flaming blush, but that would draw even more attention to them.

'If you're concerned about my welfare, I can put your mind at ease,' he said. 'I'll sleep in the room you vacated.'

'It's very flouncy and pink.'

Which was not really what she wanted to blurt out either, but there it was. Even worse, at her words the corner of his mouth twitched, as if he was trying everything he could to hold in his amusement. She almost stopped breathing. Because if this man really smiled, her heart might stutter to a halt and she'd fall dead on the floor.

'I can assure you my masculinity can handle a few flounces.'

Lucy didn't want to talk about Stefano's masculinity. Not here. Not now. Not ever. Especially not whilst he stood in this room, presenting the absolute picture of it.

'Would you like me to put your violin in front of the fire to keep it warm?'

'No, it can't take direct heat,' she said. 'Too cold and it'll crack. Too hot and dry and a similar thing will happen.'

'Temperamental, isn't it?'

'Any instrument can be if not handled correctly.'

'And do you?' He raised an eyebrow. 'Handle it correctly?'

Everything stilled at his question. Something about this moment felt pregnant and full of possibility. An idea of him and tangled limbs and the heat of two bodies exploded in her head and wouldn't leave. She glanced over at the imposing bed, and he did too. Was he thinking what she was thinking? She swallowed, her mouth dry. And even though she wore a coat, and was wrapped in a duvet, she felt completely exposed.

'I'll leave you now,' he said as he walked towards her.

She should have stepped sideways, to move out of the way of the door, but she was paralysed. Stefano stopped next to her, looming large. Hyper-real...more than a mere mortal. And this close she caught a hint of his scent. Fresh and clear, like a bright, brittle winter day in the mountains, with an intoxicating undertone of spice.

She needed to get out of the way. Instead, she took

the silk-covered duvet from around her shoulders and thrust it at him. 'You'll need this. It's from the bed.'

'*Grazie.*' He took it. In the low light of the room his dark eyes glittered as if they were filled with stars from the night sky. Then he motioned to the lock on the door and she stood to the side, looking where he indicated.

'This is the only key, if you feel the need. As I said before: you're safe here, Lucy.'

Stefano opened the door and left without looking back. Closing the door behind him, she twisted the key in the lock, which tumbled with a satisfying click.

In this moment she wasn't concerned at all about her safety. Because she'd locked the door not to keep him out. It was to keep her in.

CHAPTER FIVE

STEFANO SCANNED THE investigator's report, which contained nothing of great interest. Some of it confirmed what Lucy had already told him. That her father came from a wealthy family and had a string of failed businesses and debt behind him. Her mother was a well-respected violinist from a renowned ensemble. The obituary of her grandfather said that he was a reputed war hero with medals to prove it. No riches...nothing to hint at having profited from the sale of Lasserno's coronation ring.

Reading those words on the screen left him feeling somehow soiled and...*less*. Considering what he'd done, it was surprising he had any further to fall, but this intrusion into Lucy's life had made him do just that, and he couldn't understand why it mattered.

Still, she'd come to Lasserno and his castle for a reason. The sweet words in her letter about retracing her grandfather's steps and seeing the country made sense on the surface, but there was something deeper. A pain she hid, behind cute unicorn cat socks and glowing smiles. She might present as sunshine and rainbows, but she was more than that, he was sure.

She was off exploring the castle this afternoon—or that was what she'd texted him. After a morning when the heavenly strains of her violin had faded in and out through the castle halls. She'd played something soulful. Each perfect note sweeping over him, soothing the constant churn in his gut, the clench of his teeth, replacing it with something else. Something softer. A sense of peace.

In a way, he wished her music would never stop. But it would. The snow would melt and Lucy would leave. He didn't know why that thought ached like a mortal wound.

He shut down the document. Tried to ignore the internet alerts about the royal family. He'd once read them each day, but he didn't need to any more. Still, curiosity pricked at him, to see if the narrative had changed in the way he'd sought to achieve.

The last time he'd checked it had seemed that Alessio was releasing carefully controlled titbits to the press with the zeal of a convert. Joyous pictures of the Prince and his pregnant Princess graced the social pages in a carefully controlled way and the country loved them. Bad news had turned good. The Crown was now glorified, rather than scorned, as it had been when Alessio had first taken the throne, because of his father's antics. Suspicion of the new Prince had turned to accolades.

The twin burns of anger and regret curled tight in Stefano's gut. Those pointless thoughts invaded again. He'd been correct, no doubt. But he should never have ended up here in self-imposed exile. Alessio should have allowed his people to know the good man their Prince truly was. It was all Stefano had been trying to achieve. Except he should have fought for it rather than using subterfuge.

But there was no turning back now—only moving forward.

Stefano rubbed his hand over his face, exhaustion weighing on him like a lead blanket. He'd never required much sleep, but in recent months insomnia had been a regular and unwelcome visitor. He downed the bracing espresso he'd made earlier and settled back to search for more missing gemstones. He had a promising lead on a near flawless emerald which he would not let slip through his fingers.

As Stefano opened another email his phone rang. He checked the number. Lucy.

'*Pronto.*'

'Hi. It's…um…me.'

She still sounded uncertain when she spoke to him, which he found troubling. He wanted—*needed* her to be comfortable around him. For some strange reason it seemed imperative.

'Hello, me. How may I assist?'

She laughed, a musical tinkle of sound that caused warmth to kindle in his chest.

'I've tried following your directions to the music room, but I'm lost. I need some help.'

Her request for assistance touched him in a way he found hard to explain. He glanced at the open email again. Another contact, another phone call to make during which the person on the other end of the line would lie, whine, and then beg to be allowed to keep what wasn't theirs.

'Stefano?'

He shook himself out of his inertia. The call could wait. Helping Lucy would be a welcome break, since he'd been sitting behind this desk for hours.

'I'll find you and take you there. Can you tell me what you're near?'

'Well… I opened a door and it seems to be a room full of boars' heads. Tusks and all.'

'Ah. I won't be long.'

He shut down his computer and jogged to where she described. She stood outside the door of one of the many unused rooms here.

Today she cursed him by wearing active wear for her exploration of the castle: form-fitting leggings that peeked out from underneath her coat and clung to her body, shaping her firm thighs and the swell of her calves. Heaven save him, he couldn't take his eyes from her, and the way he looked at her body was not polite.

She gave him a tentative smile as he approached and he focussed on her soft rose lips, gleaming with a slick of gloss. It wasn't much better.

'There was no need to run. I'm fine so long as I don't open that door again.'

'I should have warned you. My father had a penchant for hunting boar. His trophies aren't to my taste, but I didn't want the boars to have perished in vain, so they now have a room to themselves.'

'You've made them their own shrine. That's kind of sweet, but also kind of creepy.'

'It is my life's aim to do "sweet and creepy" well.'

She threw back her head and laughed.

It was as if sunshine had broken out in the gloomy hall, bright and beautiful.

'Well, you're better at that than in your directions. Where is this mythical music room?'

'Follow me. You aren't far from it.'

He walked ahead and she blew out her breath in a huff, disturbing fine wisps of hair and sending them drifting over her face as she followed.

'You should have given me instructions like, *Turn right at the boars' heads, then proceed straight past the hall of disapproving ancestors and go left at the room of lethal weapons*—'

'You found the armoury as well? You *have* had an adventure today.'

'I suppose I have—though it *was* rather unnerving. What have you been doing?'

Stefano's shoulders dropped, the mere thought of the tasks ahead causing another wave of exhaustion to flood over him. 'More work.'

'I admire your commitment to your job. Do you actually have a life?'

The hot bite of something like anger burned in his gut. He'd had a life once. And status. He'd had everything. But those words came back to haunt him.

'You're nothing, Stefano, if you're not working for the Prince...'

'I had a fiancée. I had more. My work was one of service, but His Highness was my best friend.'

'Was...?'

His pace faltered, and Lucy frowned before he picked up his even stride. She was sharp, this one. Not missing anything. He couldn't admit his disgrace. What sort of a man would it make him? She'd never trust him then— not enough to divulge the secrets her family might have held when he asked her. But for some inexplicable reason he didn't want these blissful moments to end, ruined as they would be by resurrecting events in history neither of them had had any part in.

'Is.'

'Will your fiancée be coming to the castle? I don't want my being here to make things difficult.'

Celine had been reluctant to set foot in the mountains at any time. No matter that the castle was considered a national treasure, she would always say when invited here, *'I am not a goat.'*

Stefano looked over at Lucy, who was worrying her bottom lip with her teeth.

'I'm single now. Our reputations are safe.'

Lucy's expression changed, and her face became painted over with the veneer of sympathy. He'd seen that look on the face of his siblings when he'd told them about the end of his engagement. He hated it. Actions had consequences. He was living his as they spoke. He deserved no misdirected pity.

'I'm sorry,' she said. 'I know what it's like when you have an expectation of how life's going to go, and then it all just…stops.' Her eyes glittered in the low afternoon light, her voice soft and cracked with emotion.

'There's a story there,' he said.

She waved her hand, as if dismissing an irritant. 'It's a miserable one which nobody wants to hear—particularly since you sound like you have one of your own.'

'What if I do?' Strangely, he wanted to know what had chased away her smiles and laughter and replaced them with sadness.

'Let's just say I had a relationship that ended too,' Lucy murmured. Then she stopped, peered into an open doorway. 'Is this it?'

Stefano hadn't noticed where they were. He'd been too absorbed by her. 'Yes. Welcome to Castello Varno's music room.'

She walked inside as if she owned the place, and he supposed that a room like this *was* her domain. He was a mere interloper, even though it was his castle.

Lucy stood in the centre of the space and turned slowly in a circle on the parquetry floor. 'Amazing. I bet the acoustics are glorious.'

'When I was a child, my parents would have recitals here.' The room had regularly been full of people, not a silent space. Now it was an abandoned relic of a distant past.

She walked towards a piano and trailed her fingertips across the dust cover. A shiver of pleasure tripped over his skin at the thought of those gentle fingers on his flesh. Of allowing them to take a winding journey over his body. He took a step back from her. Lucy Jamieson was a risk to self-preservation and common sense.

'I'm assuming it's a concert grand?'

Stefano nodded.

'Did you ever play?' she asked.

'Not officially. My sister was taught piano, and she loathed it. For a while I took over her lessons.'

They'd been moments of true pleasure—something he'd done for himself, not about what he could give to the Arcuri royal family or his country. He'd relished those secret lessons until his teacher had reported his achievements, in a moment of pride and misplaced honesty.

'My parents stopped them. Time spent on music was considered a waste. They wanted me to only concentrate on things of use in my ultimate role.'

He couldn't prevent a sense of bitterness creeping in. It wasn't as if his marks in other subjects had diminished. His mother and father would never have known had his music teacher remained silent as he'd implored. But to them, anything that was not pertinent to his role as the future Count was unnecessary. They'd ignored the fact it was something he loved. To them, it hadn't mattered. He'd come to realise that in the end all he'd been to them was a cog in their dynasty's wheel. Not a boy who wanted one small thing to claim as his own.

A frown creased Lucy's brow. 'What did you think of that?'

'I was never going to be a musician of your skill.'

'You could take it up again.'

He shrugged. 'That chance passed me by. I had no time. I concentrated on what I needed to assist the Prince in the best way I could. History, politics, marketing, communication…'

'No wonder you're so busy. You must have a heck of a job description. What does the private secretary of a prince actually do?'

Of course he wasn't Alessio's private secretary any more, but she didn't need to know that—not right now. Let her believe that he remained in his role a little longer. It did give him a certain gravitas which 'disgraced count' lacked. How could Lucy ever trust him if he disclosed how untrustworthy he'd become?

'Anything His Highness asks of me, so long as it's legal.'

'If he asked you to…to marry the daughter of a bitter enemy to bring peace between nations?'

'Lasserno has no bitter enemies, but if he asked…' Stefano nodded. 'In centuries past, members of my family have been married off to serve the principality's interests. It made Lasserno powerful and made my family increasingly wealthy and well connected. No one complained.'

Lucy's eyes narrowed, her mouth tightening to a thin and stark line. 'That's…that's *appalling*. It doesn't sound like a best friend and employer relationship but more of a…a hostage situation.'

She seemed to grow taller, as if filled with incandescent outrage on his behalf. He'd never had anyone to support him like this. He'd always supported others. His siblings… Alessio in his role as Shield of the Crown. The burden had become a heavy one. Yet a sensation wound through him that seemed all too soft for his life right now. Almost like relief that there was someone who might think of *him*. Put him first for once.

He shut it down. Whilst he wanted to thank her for her spirited defence, those kinds of feelings led him nowhere.

'My mother and father were the product of such an arranged marriage and it was successful.' At least if politicking and building on the family's name, fortune and brand were any measure. As parents… Well, that was another matter. 'What about yours?'

She wrapped her arms round her waist, turned and looked out through the bank of windows to the cold and grey view beyond. 'Desperately in love once, apparently. Now getting bitterly divorced.'

'So love is no guarantee?'

She gave a small and savage laugh which opened the door to more questions if he cared to ask them. 'Oh, trust me, I'd *never* say it was.'

He could press…ask her about the cynicism that seemed to surround her again. Once, he would have. But now the only questions he should be asking were about her family. Her grandfather.

But he didn't have it in him to do so in this moment. Not when she seemed so lost.

Later.

He had time.

'Don't worry, Lucy. Alessio married for love. And I'm sure he'd allow the same for me, if I believed in it any more.'

'So what you're telling me is that all this is okay and you've never wanted to do anything else?'

He'd never thought of it—not even as a boy. From his first memory, his course had been set. His friendships managed. Everything that he'd done had led him to being the man he was today. Yet somehow he'd still failed.

Lucy made him question the role he'd been born into. But if he began to ask those questions they might never stop…might lead to conclusions that his life and most enduring friendship had been a lie. A hostage situation. And if that were the case, and he was now free, what was he doing tracking missing gemstones?

He had no answers to that question, which sat like an uncomfortable weight in his gut. 'I'm the Count of Varno,' he said. 'Shield of the Crown. This is my life, which I must return to.'

'Then I won't take up any more of your time,' she said, her voice barely above a whisper.

He didn't like the suspicion that Lucy believed she was being dismissed. He wanted her smiles, her laughter. Not these brittle and hard edges that seemed to have invaded their conversation.

'Tomorrow, if you like, I can take you on a proper tour.'

'That would be lovely.'

In the meantime he'd board up his weak points and slip himself back into the Count of Varno's costume. 'For now, do you think you can find your way back to familiar areas of the castle?'

'Don't worry about me. I think I know where I'm going. I'll be fine.'

Lucy turned and looked at him, her golden eyes intense and assessing. And as he left the room, to return to the work pressing down upon him, he couldn't shake the uncomfortable feeling that whilst Lucy was fine, she believed he wasn't.

CHAPTER SIX

LUCY WOKE BEFORE the alarm she'd set on her phone, snuggled deep in a warm bed, her face buried in a pillow. In a haze of early wakefulness she yawned, took a deep breath. There was the scent of sunshine. Crisp, clean sheets. And a hint of something else. An intoxicating spice, rich and deep, that teased, tempted…hit her blood and wound through her on its own seductive journey.

Stefano.

There was a reason it had been a bad idea to sleep here. His name whispered in the recesses of her consciousness. Late last night she'd imagined him lying in this bed, thought how her body touched where his had been, and now it was all she could think about. Except those thoughts had to remain just that—thoughts.

Lucy rolled over, trying to ignore the ache deep inside, the desire for things she couldn't have. Instead she stared at the canopy above her, richly embroidered with an image of the night sky. Constellations in yellows and golds. It reminded her of the few times her grandfather had taken her camping, when they'd looked up into the dark, clear night, and all they'd seen was stars. She missed those stars. The night skies in the larger cities in Europe were filled with too much light pollution to see anything very much.

When was the last time she'd simply looked up, enjoyed something so simple?

Her alarm sounded and she switched it off, checking a message from Stefano. It said he'd provided breakfast and left it outside her door and he'd meet her in the sitting room in around an hour.

She left the warmth of the bed and opened the door to the sweet scent of hot chocolate. On the floor sat a tray with a simple breakfast: some bread, butter, jam. More cheeses and meats.

Something about Stefano's thoughtfulness warmed her. It was considerate and unexpected. She needed to talk to him about the violin, but couldn't seem to find her voice. Because after spending so much time caring for herself, she was enjoying the attention more than was good for her. Plus, she still didn't really know him, and with the thick layer of snow outside she wouldn't be able to escape here any time soon if he didn't react well...

They were thoughts for another time. Today would be fun, she hoped.

Lucy ate and dressed, then made her way to Stefano, excited about his offer to show her around the castle. Her efforts the days before had kept her busy enough, but it had been like walking around a museum without any guide or information. She wanted context, and Stefano's thoughts on growing up somewhere like this, with all that history around him.

Before she rounded the corner Lucy heard him. His

voice was raised. Emotive. Speaking in Italian. She slowed her steps. Stood back a little, behind some furniture.

He came into view, pacing back and forth, raking his hand through his dark hair. His jaw was covered in stubble, as if he hadn't shaved this morning.

She didn't need to understand the words to grasp his fury. His body was wound tight, the hand clutching his phone white-knuckled, and the other hand gesticulating and slashing through the air.

Her heart bounded. That sickening twist of nerves was back in her belly. She remembered conversations like this between her parents, when her mother had been on tour, before she'd stopped touring to care for Lucy, because it had become clear her dad had no interest. Her father would rage in the late hours, when he'd thought Lucy was asleep, but she'd heard it all. Seen it, too, on the rare times she'd peeked out from her darkened room and watched her father, instead of hiding under the covers. He'd paced like this, spewing words designed to hurt a woman who was too far away to be able to do anything about it.

And just like when she was that little girl she froze, wishing she could hide, not needing to be reminded of the ugliness of her childhood. At least back then she'd been able to pretend to be asleep through the worst of it.

She really didn't have to look around the castle today with Stefano. Not when he was like this. He hadn't seen her. She could slip around the corner and leave. But as she moved he looked up, his jaw clenched, that gaze of his cold and hard.

'Back into your bed, Lucy, for Chrissakes!'

The breath left her, her heart pounding a sickening rhythm at the memory of her dad bearing down on her. Booze on his breath and hatred on his face. How could he have loved her when he'd appeared to loathe her mother so much?

She held up her hands. 'I'm sorry I'm interrupting.'

Recognition spread over Stefano's face. His eyes widened a fraction. Slashes of colour stained his cheeks. He murmured something into the phone and disconnected.

'Lucy.'

Her name was said with no trace of anger. Instead Stefano's voice ground out rough and almost pained.

'You're obviously busy,' she said. 'It's fine. We can look around the castle another day.'

She was used to changing plans. Her parents hadn't had much time for her. Her mother had often been practising or away performing once Lucy had become a little older. Her father always immersed in some hopeless scheme. Her music had been a blessing, occupying her on many lonely days when she'd suspected her parents were too wrapped up in their own misery to think about her.

'No. I have time for you, and I promised. What would you like to see first?'

His words went some way to obliterating her apprehension over the anger she'd witnessed. Her father had never been able to switch off the emotion so quickly. He was an expert at holding grudges.

'It's your home. Surprise me.'

Stefano motioned with his arm. 'Come this way.'

They began walking in silence. Lucy would have

been happy with that had it been a comfortable and companionable one. This wasn't.

She nodded to the phone, still gripped tight in his hand. 'Hard day at the office?'

Stefano looked at the mobile as if he'd just remembered he was holding it, frowned, and slid it into the pocket of his trousers. 'Sometimes people need…encouragement to do the right thing.'

They entered a long corridor. The temperature dropped here, and she assumed it was due to the bank of windows running along the right-hand side, giving an uninterrupted view of the bright snowbound landscape. It reminded her once again that whilst Stefano was treating her like an honoured guest right now, she was trapped here.

'It sounded more like evisceration than encouragement. I thought your family were supposed to be Shields of the Crown, not swords.'

'Sometimes a sword is all anyone understands. Most of my life has been spent being diplomatic. This is a new development.'

'Do you enjoy it? Being an aggressor rather than a protector?'

He looked down at her, his eyes dark and serious. 'I do what's needed.'

They stopped outside a room and, like Stefano's, she saw this door was heavily carved with a coat of arms, although different from the one on his bedroom.

'This crest isn't yours?'

'No,' he said. 'It's the royal family's.'

'It hasn't got a unicorn rampant either. I call it inferior.'

The corner of his mouth twitched. 'I invite you to tell His Highness. I suspect he'll disagree.'

Before she left the castle she'd get him to smile. But when she did, it would have to be immediately before she walked out through the door, because she was sure his smile would have the capacity to devastate her.

'Why do they get a coat of arms here?'

'This suite's reserved exclusively for Lasserno's royal family.'

'Lucky them. Does the Moretti family get a suite in the palace in return?'

Stefano shrugged. 'I don't stay in the palace. I have a home in the capital.'

That wasn't what she'd asked, but she let it slide. He opened the door and flicked on the lights as they went inside.

'Wow.'

Glittering chandeliers hung from a ceiling which seemed to writhe with frescoes. A heavenly sky…angels blowing trumpets. Thankfully no more gruesome scenes like those she'd come across in other areas of the castle. She didn't need any more reminding of her own mortality. In this room, everywhere she looked something gleamed with the rich burnish of gold.

'Indeed. It's the grandest room in the castle.'

It was all a bit…*much*. 'Do you actually like it?'

Stefano stood in the centre of the room, looking up. 'It's of its time. The whole castle is—though this was a more recent renovation, from the eighteenth century. I find it somewhat extravagant.'

'I was raised in a house in the suburbs.' She tried to stifle a giggle, unsuccessfully. This was so far from where she'd come from. 'You live in a *castle*, Stefano. I think you've cornered the market on extravagance.'

He sighed. 'My apologies. This is my life; it's normal to me. But some days I feel more a custodian of history rather than a true resident.'

'I'm not sure I could sleep in here, with all those angels heralding my divine right to rule and my hereditary magnificence.'

'Most royalty enjoy their own magnificence a little too much.'

'What about Lasserno's current Prince?'

Stefano's mouth tightened and a muscle in his jaw ticked. 'He's a good man.'

There was a world of pain in his expression. She knew about wounds that were kept well-hidden, considering she had a few of her own.

'You should explore,' Stefano said. 'Treat the room like you own it.'

Lucy smiled. 'That's a loaded invitation. You never know what I'll get up to.'

He seemed wound so tight and tense, that she wanted to loosen him up a bit. Untie those mental knots that kept him so firmly bound. She walked through to a bathroom, with bright mosaic tiles on the floor, gilt mirrors, a shower which appeared to be a newer addition. But it was the huge bath which would fit four people easily that grabbed her full attention.

She went to it, peered inside. 'It's hand-painted. With fish and mermaids.' She turned to Stefano. 'Your bath isn't.'

'Praise all things holy. I might become self-conscious,

being watched by all those judgemental eyes. Especially the mermaids. Their standards appear…high.'

She had to admit they did look rather judgemental.

'I don't think you have anything to be self-conscious about.'

Stefano raised an eyebrow. 'Really?'

There was a silence again, but this silence wasn't uncomfortable. It was full of things left unsaid. He seemed looser, his gaze softer as he looked at the bath, then at her. She could imagine him lying there, his warm brown skin slick in the water. The feel of him…two bodies sliding together limbs entwined…

Lucy's cheeks heated. 'You *know* you don't.'

His dark eyes twinkled. Again, he wasn't smiling as such, but there was no mistaking the fact that he was…amused.

'Please tell me—I'd appreciate your insight.'

She waved her hand up and down, generally indicating his glorious body. 'Tall, dark, handsome count with a castle. Really, Stefano. You're the perfect cliché.'

His mouth curled and broke into a blinding smile, and then he chuckled, the deep, throaty sound rolling right through her in a wave of heat that warmed her way better than any fire. It was sweeter than the hot chocolate he'd made for her. She wanted to kiss that mouth…the crinkles at the corners of his eyes…as the whole of him stopped looking dark and brooding and simply blazed like the sun.

She was weak for him. Stefano made her as gooey inside as the marshmallows she'd fantasised about toasting. She had to get away. Because if she didn't, she might beg him to kiss her.

She scurried from the bathroom and went through another door. Stefano followed. She could tell he was close from the way goosebumps shimmied up and down her spine at his palpable presence. The next room she walked into was the royal bedroom, with a huge bed covered in a rich blue velvet and gold-embossed pillows. Even worse than the bathroom.

'Have you ever been in here and been tempted to break some unwritten rules?'

'Lucy, what are you asking?'

A wry grin played on his lips. It was a good look on him. It seemed impossible that he could become any more handsome till he'd smiled. Then he became devastating.

'I don't know… Did you ever jump on the bed as a child?'

He put his hand to his heart, his expression earnest, but she knew he was playing along. 'I would never have dared. But how would *you* like to feel like royalty?'

'What do you mean?'

Stefano looked at the bed. Looked at her. Cocked his eyebrow. 'I won't tell anyone if you want to try out the bed.'

Lucy grinned. She couldn't help herself. Her heart beat faster with the thrill of it all. 'Okay, but I won't jump on it. I promise. Kind of…'

She toed off her shoes and climbed onto the soft velvet cover. Flopped down on her back and made the shape of a starfish.

'What do you think?' he asked.

'Why don't you try it out for yourself?' She patted the bed beside her.

He started forward, then hesitated.

'You know you want to… *Your Excellency.*'

Stefano kicked off his shoes as well. Lucy straightened herself out and allowed some room for him as he lay down too, in a dignified, manly kind of way. No flopping to be seen.

He let out a long, slow breath. Moved about a bit as if trying out the mattress. 'I like mine better.'

Even though the bed was enormous, lying there with Stefano was still too close. Lucy closed her eyes for a moment, tried to shut him out as they lay in silence, but she still caught a hint of him. A scent like warm spice. That smell had invaded her dreams, as had the man himself. And, whilst she couldn't really remember what had actually happened in them, all she knew was that she'd woken up with the sheets tangled round her legs, the whole bed in disarray, and a delicious warmth sliding through her.

'I think that I prefer your bed too.'

Lucy opened her eyes. Her voice didn't sound like her own. More of a sultry whisper than a statement of fact. Stefano turned his head, his dark eyes blacker than usual, the pupils drowning out the espresso-brown. Her heart thumped. That familiar rush of heat which she'd woken up to was now rushing through her. Enticing. Intoxicating. She knew what it was—desire. And she couldn't, *shouldn't* desire this man. Not when her life was such a mess. Especially not when she was keeping secrets from him.

Then his lips parted, his fingers flexing on the coverlet. The moment swelled with possibility.

'What do you like about my bed, Lucy?'

The smell of you. Imagining you in it naked. With me.
But she couldn't say any of those things.

'The canopy. The constellations. I miss seeing the stars for real. There's too much light in the big cities here.'

A look passed across his face. Stark, blank…almost hopeless. Stefano turned his head to stare up at the ceiling. Then he sat up, ran his hand through his hair. 'The castle's large, and there's much more to show you.'

She regretted the change in mood. That she hadn't taken a leap of faith and told him what she really felt. But she wasn't sure she could trust him. She hardly trusted herself.

'I promise I won't have you breaking any more rules,' she said. 'Even though I think you kind of enjoyed it.'

The corner of his mouth kicked up in another wry kind of grin which made him look younger, almost devilish, and her silly heart tripped over itself.

'It's one more sin to add to a list of many,' he said.

Yet despite that lightness his voice carried a weight heavy enough to break a person. She wanted to reach out, clasp his hand, ask what was wrong, but she wasn't sure he'd accept it or give her an honest answer.

Instead, Lucy slid off the bed. She straightened the crushed covers and dented pillows as he did the same on his side. Their movements struck her as intensely intimate and domestic.

She swallowed, her mouth dry. 'Where to now?'

'Perhaps the portrait gallery, so you can view the members of my noble family?'

She didn't want to see that—all those pictures of his deceased and judgemental relatives. She wanted to know more about *him*, the man, with a ferocity that completely overtook her.

'Do you have a favourite place here? One you love more than anywhere else?'

'*Sì.*'

'Then take me there.'

He needed to get out of here. Escape this room. Lying down next to her had been a mistake. Not because he was concerned that only the bodies of royalty should lie in the hallowed bed they'd lain on together—that was the flimsy lie he'd told himself. It was more.

The naked avalanche of desire that had struck and mown him down, crushing his will. Seeing her lying on that royal bed, with her strawberry blonde hair spilling over the pillows, he hadn't been able to help but think of her in *his* bed. Which had led to inevitable thoughts of being in that bed with her.

It had been all he could do when they'd lain on the pristine covers not to invite her into his arms. Kiss her. Evoke soft moans of pleasure as he made love to her, burying himself in the warmth of Lucy's body and forgetting everything. But forgetting wasn't an option. Not for him. He needed to remember, to dwell on his pain. Because he hadn't served his penance yet and might never do so.

He went to the door of the Royal Suite. She wanted to know his favourite place here? He'd show her. That was safer than this fever which gripped him in its thrall.

They walked together through some of the service corridors, utilitarian spaces of rough-hewn stone and little embellishment.

'I don't know how you find your way around,' said Lucy. 'Do you ever get lost?'

Stefano looked over at her. Her cheeks were red. She seemed a little puffed.

He adjusted his stride and slowed down for her. 'As children we ran wild in this place.'

'A game of hide and seek must have been impossible. You'd never find each other.'

'Mainly we hid from the nanny and our lessons. But I came away with an excellent mental map of the castle.'

'Where were your mum and dad?'

'Politicking. Their favourite pastime. Here we are.'

He grabbed the hem of his sweater and pulled it over his head. Dropped it on a chair outside some double doors. The chill of the air on this side of the castle was an immediate shock after the warmth of his clothing.

'What are you doing?' Lucy asked.

She was staring at him with a mixture of surprise that he should be undressing in the cold, and something else. With her eyes a little wider, and her mouth in an unspoken *oh*, it looked a lot like…fascination.

He preferred her looking at him like this, with a kind of wonder on her face. Not the way she'd been earlier, when her eyes had been wide with trepidation. Stefano hadn't wanted Lucy to witness his ugliness, what he'd become in his pursuit of redemption. It was important that she think well of him, and he didn't stop to analyse why.

'Trust me when I say you won't need your coat here.'

Lucy narrowed her eyes, but she shrugged her coat off, dropped it on the chair over his sweater. Her long-sleeved knit top hugged her figure, gave him a tantalising glimpse of her slender waist, the perfect swell of her breasts. She was his guest—in his care. He shouldn't be lusting over her. But she was all beauty and sunshine and he craved the light.

She wrapped her arms round her waist. Bounced up and down on her toes. 'Okay, I'm officially freezing.'

'You won't be for long.'

He pushed the double doors open into an entrance hall. A rich, earthy smell permeated the space. The temperature here was warmer, the air more humid.

Lucy relaxed a little, her arms looser by her side as she seemed to unknot. 'Where *are* we?'

Stefano smiled. 'One of the castle's greatest treasures.'

He walked towards some glass doors which were fogged, with rivulets of moisture running down the inside, and opened them. Heat and humidity blasted them like a palpable hit from the expansive tropical conservatory. Full of palms and ferns, it was a wonder of his mountain home. Even though he'd been here numerous times, it never failed to amaze him.

'This is incredible,' Lucy said, her voice full of breathless wonder. 'I can't believe the castle has somewhere like *this*.'

Condensation covered the glass, so it was difficult to see outside. On the days when you could it was a kind of magic, standing in the tropics whilst the world outside lay gripped in the depths of winter.

'One of my ancestors was a renowned horticulturalist who designed and built a famed Italian-style garden at the palace. But his first love was the tropics. He sought to create the same here. In many ways, this conservatory was considered his folly.'

It's what had prompted his brother to study horticulture. As children they'd spent so much time here, paddling in the tropical pond, hiding in the ferns. On returning from the capital, it had always been the first place in the castle Stefano visited after speaking with the staff. Whenever he walked in here, breathed the warm air, it was as if all the stress he carried was untangled.

Perspiration pricked at the back of Stefano's neck. It wouldn't be long before it was too hot in here for either of them, wearing all their winter clothing.

As if reading his mind, Lucy peeled off her long-sleeved top, leaving herself in a clinging strappy undershirt, with a shadow of perspiration at her lower back.

Palms fanned out overhead, the whole place lush and fertile. The only sound in the space was the crunch of Lucy's boots on the gravel path and the plink of water dripping into the pond.

'It's almost like the rainforest I went bushwalking in as a child...'

She turned to him and held her arms out wide, looking up at a tree fern like a huge green umbrella above them. A few droplets of condensation from its fronds dripped on her face.

She smiled, wiped them away. 'Who looks after all this?'

'It's my brother's project now. Some gardeners help, but I sent them home with the rest of the staff. Most of the water is controlled by computer, but Gino tells me what else is needed. He asks for photographs of the plants that worry him. Sometimes I'll hand-water, if what's provided by the sprinkler system isn't enough.'

'I can't believe you don't spend all your time here. It's almost like you're punishing yourself, living this ascetic life in a few cold rooms.'

How close she was to the truth. 'I'd hardly call living in a castle "ascetic". You said it was extravagant.'

She narrowed her eyes. 'You're being obtuse and know exactly what I mean.'

What would she think of him if she discovered the full extent of how far he'd fallen? He didn't know why that thought filled him with dread.

Luckily, she didn't question him any further. Instead, Lucy walked towards the pond, trailed her hands through the water which, from experience, he knew would be warm. He was only sorry the water lilies weren't in bloom. Lucy would love the water lilies.

'Why is the temperature in the rest of the castle so cold when in here it's like this?'

'If the temperature falls in this place, it will all die.' After everything else he'd done, he would not lose this too. 'What does it matter if I'm cold? To protect it until Bruno can repair the heating, I'm diverting most of the resources to the conservatory.'

She frowned. 'You're diverting some to me too. I should go and leave you be. Not add to your worries.'

'You're welcome here, Lucy. And I don't want you to leave until I've heard you play.'

She pressed the thumb of her right hand deep into her left palm and rubbed, staring into the distance. He wondered if she even knew she was doing it—the action seemed almost reflexive. She moved further into the space, gently brushing aside some plants hanging across her path.

'This is such a special place…'

'It's where I proposed to my fiancée.'

He didn't know why he'd made that admission. It was one of the reasons he only came here out of necessity lately—although with Lucy's presence the pain of the memory seemed somehow distant. Not so bright and fresh…more like a sun-faded photograph.

'Thank you for bringing me here, then. It must be hard, with those memories. Especially since this is your favourite place in the castle.'

When he'd planned his proposal his intention had been to take Celine to a tropical island, chasing summer. But Alessio's father had abdicated, throwing Lasserno into crisis. Instead he'd brought her here, because the conservatory had always seemed to him like another world.

'She didn't really like it. Said the humidity made her hair kink.'

Lucy stared at him but said nothing, and he appreciated her silence. He noted that in the humidity her hair had developed a distinctive curl to it. She didn't seem to mind—or perhaps she didn't even notice.

Lucy strolled back towards him, a fine sheen of perspiration across her skin, making her gleam. 'I hope you don't mind me asking, but why did your engagement end?'

The real truth he couldn't admit. He wouldn't have Lucy thinking less of him—not when in this moment he felt as if life had some hope again. The sensation would fade soon enough, when reality intruded, but for now he wanted this. To keep it and hold it for himself. Where was the harm?

He shrugged. 'I've taken a…a step back from my role as His Highness's secretary to repair the castle. My fiancée liked my status and links to the Crown more than she liked me.'

Lucy's eyes widened. 'Gosh, I'd marry you for the conservatory alone. Who cares about a prince?'

Laughter burst from her. The joy on her face was infectious. He couldn't help himself. He laughed too. She did that to him—brought back the connection to his humanity when before it was as if he'd forgotten how to have fun. And that feeling—the shining light of happiness and his enjoyment of Lucy's company—flared inside him, strong and bright.

'You're worth more, you know,' she said. 'You're not your work. No one is.'

His role was all he had. All he'd been born to. All he'd aspired to. All he'd ever wanted. He and Alessio against the world, carving their own path. But he wondered now, as he watched Lucy nibbling on her lower lip with an inward-looking expression on her face, whether she'd been speaking to him or herself.

'How would you know?' he asked.

She seemed to shake herself from that introspection and come back to him.

'You're dedicated to what appears to be an unpleasant job right now. You're here in the castle on your own, freezing yourself, making sure that the conservatory your brother loves stays alive. You've taken me in—some muddy stranger on your doorstep. You seem like a good man, and finding a good man is hard.'

'I'm simply a man, Lucy. More flawed than most, I promise you.'

It was a warning to her not to get close. A reminder to himself not to forget who he was and what he had to do here—even if the reasons seemed to be a little fuzzy and out of focus today.

'My mother says that if you break up with some-one you should reclaim the places you went together as a couple just for yourself. To own them again. I did that after…'

'After you broke up with your boyfriend?'

She let out a deep and heavy sigh. 'After I found my ex-boyfriend in bed with another member of the orchestra. A pretty young viola player.'

A hot burst of anger roared through him like a flash fire. How could anyone do that to her, especially some-one he supposed she'd loved?

'You're a beautiful young violinist, and he was a fool.'

Her lips turned up in a soft smile, but her eyes remained sad. 'Thank you. I'm trying to think that, but it's been hard. At least we weren't engaged. But the point of this isn't to get sympathy for myself. There was a little café in Salzburg we used to go to during rehearsals. It sold the best pastries. Just before I came here, I went there. Ordered a coffee and cake and sat. Enjoyed it on my own. I took the café back. That's what *you* need to do—make new memories for yourself.'

'Perhaps I will.'

She was so bright—like one of the vibrant orchids which bloomed here. A splash of colour in all the green.

Any thoughts associated with this place would now seem full of her.

'What would it take for me to capture good memories here, to reclaim this space, Lucy?'

She hesitated. 'I—I don't know. But…something momentous?'

Her face and cheeks flushed the colour of a newly opened rose. She looked like summer, standing there in her strappy top, with the bare skin of her arms exposed and pale. Everything here smelled raw, like life and earth, except for her. Lucy was the delicate hint of flowers. She wasn't merely beautiful, but achingly so. The warm gold of her eyes glowing in the light.

All Stefano could think about now was the pout of her exquisite mouth…how he wanted to run his thumb over her lower lip to see if it was as soft as it appeared. He reached out. Hesitated a moment. She didn't move away. Instead, she leaned into him. He drifted his thumb over that perfect lower lip and it was as silky as he had imagined. Her eyes fluttered closed, her eyelashes fanning over her cheeks.

A kiss would do it—chase away any remaining memories of a day that was supposed to be special and instead had somehow *lacked*. But kissing Lucy would be wrong. It would be madness. And still he stepped towards her, eased his arms around her waist.

Her eyes opened, then widened, and she slid the palms of her hands flat on his chest, splaying her fingers over his muscles. A tremor ran through her. Not cold, but goosebumps, which peppered her skin under his fingers. He dropped his head and she rose to meet him.

The merest brush of their mouths and he was lost.

Lucy was black ice. She was danger. Someone who diverted him from what he needed to do, from what was right. And yet he didn't care. Instead, he let go. Allowed himself to slip and to fall.

A flame of desire ignited and took hold.

Lucy made a sound, almost pained, pressed harder into his body as if she couldn't get close enough. So he tightened his arms till there was no space between them. Her lips parted under his as their tongues touched, slipped over one another.

It didn't seem like a first kiss, where two people needed to learn one another. This was more knowing. A passionate give and take. Nothing tentative. A kiss driven only by instinct.

Stefano was hard, aching. Almost desperate. He should stop, but the kiss only deepened. She must know—she'd have to feel his need, pressed together as they were. Still, she didn't pull away, and he hoped she never would. This was desire in its purest form—a welcoming of two bodies together in perfect harmony. They shouldn't, but he wanted to have her here. Except there was nowhere to lie. And this was a woman who deserved a bed with soft covers and crisp sheets. Not ravishment on a garden bench or moist earth.

His mind catalogued the places close by. He could swoop her into his arms, take her back to the Royal Suite and make love to her there...

Then he noticed her slowing, pulling away. He wanted to chase the kiss. Fight for it. But instead he stopped and pulled back too, even though inside he howled like a wild animal. He looked down at her lips, plump and red. Her breath coming in heavy gusts, mirroring his own. He loosened his arms, even though he wanted to tell her she should never leave them.

'I…' It was as if Lucy couldn't get out any words. Her eyes were glazed, her pupils wide. Her dumbfounded look mirrored how he felt.

'If that's not what you wanted, I'm sorr—'

'No. It was perfect…' She raised a trembling hand to her mouth. 'The perfect way for you to take this place back. I'm glad I could…help.'

Lucy stepped away from him.

He knew he should stop her, but she turned and fled.

Stefano could do nothing but let her go.

CHAPTER SEVEN

Lucy looked out of the window of Stefano's room. The sun was out, the snow no longer falling. She'd had dinner in here last night, after getting a text saying he had to work and would leave a meal in the kitchen for her. She'd welcomed the breakfast tray he'd dropped outside her door this morning, giving her some space. Apart from texts, they hadn't spoken at all.

Did he regret what had happened?

She lifted her fingers to her lips and closed her eyes, revisiting the kiss that had kept her awake half the night. The pleasure of it was still humming through her veins. How she'd never wanted it to stop, but known it *had* to.

She still hadn't told him about the violin, and something about keeping that secret now didn't feel right. When she'd first arrived, she hadn't been sure of him and how he might react to what she had to say. Now she didn't want to ruin this growing understanding between them that was as confusing as it was precious.

Only the pure force of the iron will which helped her practise through boredom and sometimes pain had her running away from Stefano in the conservatory as if their kiss had meant nothing but a mere favour. Who was she kidding? It hadn't done any favours for her. It had rocked her world.

Lucy wasn't sure what it had done for Stefano. She wasn't completely naïve. He'd been hard. Aroused. But she figured that simply happened when a man got up close and personal with any woman. And maybe when she'd stepped back he might have had a confused look, as if he'd taken a hard knock to the head, but she didn't really know. She hadn't been thinking very clearly herself.

Which was why she was here with her violin, looking to play. It grounded her, losing herself in the music. Reminded her of who she really was. Trying to achieve the perfect pitch and those notes that sang through her and her instrument so she could forget the wallop of passion she hadn't realised could exist between two people.

In her limited experience, with only one boyfriend, it had never occurred to her that there was something in the world better than the feeling she could get from her playing. But Stefano's lips on hers had eclipsed it all, and they'd been fully clothed. She'd never wanted the moment to end.

Lucy tried to ignore the wicked hum inside that tempted her to think of him less…*dressed*. She couldn't. Wouldn't. Some might say that thoughts were free, but that kind of thinking would take her nowhere.

Lucy started with the exercises her physiotherapist had told her to work on, warming up her hands and gently stretching them before picking up her violin, her bow. So familiar they were like old friends, like part of her. She played some simple scales first. Her fingers might be a bit stiff but there was no pain today, so she started a more complicated exercise.

When she'd finished a knock sounded at the door. Soft, not a demand, more a polite request to enter.

Her heart rate jumped from *lento* to *presto*, and it was only luck and good fortune that stopped her bow slipping from her fingers and falling to the floor.

'Come in.' Her voice sounded thready and faint. She swallowed as the door eased open.

Stefano entered the room slowly, as if he wasn't sure what would greet him. She supposed she had fled from him and the conservatory the day before like a vampire trying to escape dawn. It hadn't been a dignified exit.

He stood there in his usual clothing. Jeans, boots, sweater. Effortlessly casual and artfully dishevelled. She, on the other hand, was a mish-mash of figure-hugging active wear and a warm pullover that had seen better days but was soft and warm as a hug.

It didn't seem to matter to Stefano. He looked at her as if she was a steaming cup of coffee after a long, sleepless night. How she wanted him to drink her right down. And all she could think about now was the contrasts of him. Hard body, gentle lips, a kiss that stopped time...

'Please. I heard the music,' he said. 'You don't have to stop for me.'

Lucy tried not to think about how perfect it had been, having his arms wrapped tight around her. 'I was only practising a little.'

'Would you play something?'

'I don't have any accompaniment.'

It was a cop-out. She didn't need a soundtrack. What stopped her was the nerves churning in her belly like that hive of bees again, intent on stinging her. She wanted to know what he thought—whether the kiss had stunned him as much as it had her. It shouldn't matter, but somehow his approval seemed vital. Because something had changed in those moments in the conservatory. Things she couldn't give voice to.

'If you did, what would you play for me?'

Light filtered through the mullioned windows. Outside the landscape lay crisp, cold and perfect. That pristine beauty masked a creeping danger to those who were unwary. And that sense of hidden peril was a lot like the way she'd come to view love—though why *that* word should enter her head now she didn't know.

'Vivaldi. *Four Seasons*. "Winter".'

Stefano pulled his cell phone from his pocket and smiled. 'For a woman who hates winter, you have an affinity for it.'

'I can admit it looks pretty,' she said, as he unlocked his phone and began scrolling through. 'You know my feelings otherwise.'

He raised a dark, perfect eyebrow. 'Are you comfortable here?'

The question was a loaded one, but gently asked. She gave a truthful answer. 'I am, thank you.'

Lucy wasn't apprehensive the way she had been in the beginning. She was more afraid of herself and her feelings, which seemed to want to leak out all over the place—especially all over him.

He nodded, and something about him relaxed. His stance appeared a little looser, as if he'd been worried before and was not so much now.

After a few short minutes Stefano seemed to find what he was looking for and held up his phone with the screen facing her. 'Is this you?'

She walked forward, peered at the screen. It was a video of her charity performance with a string ensemble a few years earlier. She swallowed through the knot in her throat. 'Yes.'

His lips curled into a smile. 'Then we have accompanying music—of sorts. I can cast the sound to the speakers here. I would love to hear you. The snow's stopped falling. If it stays that way, the roads will be clear soon enough.'

Meaning she'd be able to go. Walk away from here and never see him again. She didn't know why that thought hurt. But this was a wish she could grant for the kindness he had shown her. She'd needed a soft landing after all she'd been through, and even though he might not have realised Stefano had given her that.

'Okay. That should work.'

She would be better than the performance on video, so that would compensate for her lack of practice. She could do this. It would be just like playing along, and the background sound would hide any stumbles from the fingers that still didn't work so well.

Stefano walked to an armchair in front of the fire and sat. 'Ready?'

She took a few moments, a deep breath in, a slow exhalation, settling the churn in her belly. Something more than the normal apprehension she might experience before a concert. It was as if this performance was the most important of her life. The need gripped her to be perfect for him, an audience of one.

Lucy positioned her violin, her bow. Nodded. He pressed play and there was a pregnant silence before the staccato sound of strings filled the room. His eyes were on her, intent, as Lucy waited in those thrilling moments full of expectation before she struck the first notes of flawless sound, vibrating through her and her instrument. It settled the cracking nerves, soothed the bumps of fear. And then that sense of release overwhelmed her, and she was nothing but the flow of sound as her fingers worked and she drew her bow across the strings. Immersed in her playing, ceasing to exist bar a pinprick of consciousness where the music became everything.

But all the while she knew.

Something about this was different.

It was more than the joy of the music. She played for *him*—Stefano. All the words left unsaid after their kiss in the conservatory were poured into her playing, and she hoped he heard what she'd been unable to voice, what the music allowed her to feel. Hoped he had the sense that she'd shared part of her soul with him.

Then she closed her eyes, let the memory of their perfect kiss wash over her, flood her playing, and sank into the music and her message, allowing herself to be carried away.

As patron of Lasserno's orchestra Stefano had seen a great deal of music performed live before, by some of the best musicians on the planet. He was privileged in that regard. But this was something else…having music played for him alone by Lucy.

It was a revelation.

He couldn't take his eyes from her… He felt the intimacy of this moment as he had in those perfect seconds as their lips had touched the day before. When he'd thought there could be nothing much better in the world than the way his need for her had hit his blood like a shot of spirits.

It was like that now, watching her play her violin. Her eyes half closed. Her face serene at times, agonised at others. He became immersed in the music as each note struck him, like an arrow to the chest. The sound embedded inside him, swelling and growing till the passion in her playing filled him.

It could crack you in two this music. How could someone take wood and strings and create a sound like from heaven?

In those moments it filled him to overflowing, as if the emotions in the music would spill out of him too. Lucy's performance—the brilliance of her—had stolen his voice. His breath. It had stolen everything. He was lost in her. The perfect sound reverberated from the walls, flooded through him as if it could cleanse his very soul. He'd experienced many things in life. Beauty, pleasure, joy. But nothing could eclipse these moments now, when she played for him. It was as if every note carried a message, inscribed on his soul in permanent ink. An indelible mark.

Then, in a flurry of brilliance, fingers and bow, the music ended too soon. The crowd on the video applauded and he wished he could provide a true crowd here, to fete the genius he'd witnessed. But there was only him. Unworthy in all ways. He still clapped, though, because what more could he do? She deserved the accolades, the cheers of *Bravo!* that the audience on the video provided for her in a standing ovation.

He stood as well, whilst she clutched her violin with a beatific smile and bowed. Colour sat high on her cheeks. She breathed hard, looking like a woman who had experienced ecstasy.

In a blinding moment he wished he'd been the one to put that look on her face.

'You're magnificent,' he said. His voice didn't sound like his own. It was strangely hollow, almost as if he were speaking outside himself.

'Thank you. I haven't performed for a while. I made some mistakes.'

'I would never have guessed. I don't know how you do it.'

He approached her and she looked up at him, glowing. 'Easy. Fingers. Bow. Practice.'

'Don't undersell yourself. What you do is *not* easy. I wouldn't be able to play a single note.'

'Of course you could. I could show you.'

He looked at the precious instrument which she held so lightly in her brilliant hands. Stefano knew the value of a violin so old—both in monetary terms and to a performer like her. She'd been willing to sleep with it to prevent it getting too cold. To let him touch it...?

'One note?' he said.

She smiled, and the warmth of her happiness filled him with the same joy as if she was still playing her violin for him.

'We'll start with the bow. Thumb here in the space.' She showed him and it looked effortless. A light touch which created magic. 'Middle fingers curled over. Tip of the little finger on the top of the bow.'

Lucy gave the bow to him and Stefano followed her instructions.

She nodded. 'Pretty good. Now, take the violin and hold it firmly round the neck.'

She held it out to him and he grasped the wood, still warm from her hand, as she circled round behind him.

'Don't drop it, but don't throttle it either.'

Her voice was close, and he could still hear the smile in it.

'Stand with your feet shoulder-width apart and relax.'

'I'm holding the three-hundred-year-old instrument of a renowned violinist, Lucy. I'm unable to *relax*.'

That, and he could sense her warmth. The knowledge of her standing close was sending a shiver down his spine.

She snorted. 'Fair point. Now, put the violin on the top of your shoulder, cheek and chin on the rest, try not to tense up…'

He simply listened to her lilting voice, followed what she told him to do.

'I just need to adjust you a bit, okay?' she said.

'Of course.'

Her hands were on him then, and he was captive to her gentle touch, changing his position. Hers to move however she pleased as she murmured words of encouragement. He lost himself in her, forgetting about the valuable instrument he held, focussed entirely on her because nothing else existed. He wondered if anything ever would again after this. It was as if the longer she was here, the more she was changing him.

Lucy stood back a little, inspected him. 'You're perfect.'

He wished he was...but that man didn't exist any more. Still, he would pretend—for her.

She approached again, from the front. 'Now, draw the bow across the strings.'

Stefano did, and the violin gave an unearthly screech. He stopped immediately.

Lucy laughed. 'Everyone does that the first time they play—even me. It's not about failing; it's about not giving up. Here.'

She adjusted the bow's position a fraction, her fingers warm on his skin.

'Try again.'

He did, and the note reverberated through him, a clear, crisp sound. One. Perfect. Note.

'You did it!'

Her smile was like the midday sun hitting snowfall. It blinded him.

'A beautifully played D! I know it's not a piano, but you said you'd always wanted to play an instrument. Maybe you can learn?'

He handed her back the violin, her bow, and she did what she needed to with them before placing them safely back in the case.

'Thank you.'

His voice sounded cracked. He'd enjoyed many advantages of his birth, his position, but of all the things he'd been able to do this moved him more than any other. Her thoughtfulness, everything about her, called to him. All he wanted to do was reach out…touch. Let her brilliance cleanse him of his many sins.

Lucy shifted her violin out of the way and flexed her hand. Pressed her thumb deep into her palm.

'You do that often,' he said.

She shrugged. 'I suffered an injury and I've had to rest it. But since I've been here it hasn't been too bad.'

'And I asked you to play for me. I'm sorry. I didn't know.'

She'd been reluctant to play when he'd asked and perhaps this was the reason why.

'It was good. I've been at a…a crossroads. Playing hasn't been as joyful as it once was. I've been wondering if I should stop—but then who would I be?'

It was a terrifyingly familiar sentiment.

Lucy continued working her thumb into her wrist and then into her forearm. He hoped her playing today hadn't hurt her. If it had, it was just another thing to feel guilty for.

Stefano reached out to her, hesitated. 'May I?'

Lucy held out her hand, palm up. He took it, cradled it in his own. The tips of her fingers were flushed pink. He brushed his own over them, then her palm. She gave a sharp exhalation.

'Do they hurt?' he asked.

'Not for a long time. I have calluses there now.'

Her voice was a whisper as he touched her skin and held the true instrument of her brilliance—not the violin, but her hands. He stroked his finger along her palm, then down each of her fingers. The pupils of her golden eyes flared wide and dark.

'Who would think that flesh and bone could contain such skill?'

'I've worked hard and my body's suffering for it.'

'Is it painful right now?' He pressed his own thumb where he'd seen hers go so often during her short stay here.

She moaned softly. 'You're strong. Better than my physiotherapist.' She looked up at him. 'That feels so good.'

He shouldn't be this close to her. He shouldn't be touching her. Because all he wanted to do was kiss her pain away. Their kiss in the conservatory had been a revelation. Lucy in his arms…confusing everything that he'd thought he wanted or needed. The way they'd fitted together so perfectly had made him question his place, where he should be—because now there was no more important place than here. In the mountains of his ancestral home. Alone with Lucy and her music.

The sound of it had awakened something in him—as though for years he'd been walking through a fog and then she'd entered his life and it had lifted to reveal a brilliant, sunny day he hadn't realised existed. Burned off the mist of despair to give him something dangerous, like hope. Hope that underneath—somewhere buried deep—he was still a good man.

'You are a miracle,' he whispered.

He took her hand and placed it on the flat of his chest, his own hand over hers. The warmth of her palm almost burned through his clothes. She looked up at him, her lips parted, cheeks still flushed a sunset-pink. The pupils of her eyes were wide and dark, almost obliterating the warm honey-brown.

'Not a miracle…just a woman.'

'No, you're more.'

He cupped her jaw with his free hand and lowered his mouth to hers. She met him halfway. Their lips touched and it was if something inside them exploded as they burst into life. She slid her hands up, over his shoulders and into his hair, gripping tight as if never wanting to let him go. He wound his arms around her, pressing her into him. Her body against his was still the perfect fit.

The fire crackled low in the hearth, warming the room, filling it with a dusky glow. There was no one here but her and him…two people shipwrecked together. The world would exist again soon enough, but today he needed to pretend. His whole life had been set out for him, directed as if it were a play and he a mere actor. Lucy wasn't written into any script, but for once he craved to do what he wanted rather than what was required of him.

Lucy was unexpected. A bright, perfect burst of passion in what had otherwise been a passionless life—one of duty and honour but somehow *lacking*. He hadn't seen it before, but he knew it now, with brutal clarity as he held this woman in his arms and simply allowed himself to *want*. Nothing would intrude—not his duty to his siblings, not recovering the Crown Jewels. For now he was simply Stefano Moretti the man. Not His Excellency the Count of Varno, Shield of the Crown.

He slowed the kiss before passion completely overtook him…pulled back. Lucy made a muffled sound of protest.

'I crave you, Lucy. Crave to make love to you and to hell with tomorrow. Tell me you want that too.'

She looked up at him, her lips a deep blush-pink, her golden eyes searching his face. She wasn't pushing him away, but he loosened his arms nonetheless. Stefano recognised the disparity of their positions. He didn't want her to feel beholden to him, for giving her shelter in the castle. He was in the position of power, but he needed her to know she had all the control.

'If you don't want what I do I'll walk away. You've nothing to fear.'

The corners of her perfect mouth tilted as she threaded her hands into his hair once more. His heart thumped hard and fast, beating in his chest like timpani.

'I'm not afraid of you.' Her voice was soft, like the sound of the world in the moments before snow fell. 'Take me to bed, Stefano.'

He groaned and swept her into his arms. Her lips had parted and her eyes were bright with a glorious flame. He walked the short distance to his bed, placed her gently on the covers. She needed care, reverence, this woman who played like an angel and injured herself for her art.

That heady drumbeat in his chest drove him, spurred him onwards. But he was tired of a life that was hard and fast. All he craved was softness.

He kicked off his shoes, lay over her. Lucy's body was supple and pliant under him. She parted her legs and he settled between them, resting in her warmth, aching with desire. He dropped his lips to hers again and she welcomed him. Their tongues touched and he was lost. The scent of her was rich, like raspberries and cream. Like the perfect dessert at the end of a meal. It was a promise of something that might be out of reach for ever, but for today was his to grasp.

He slid a hand under her top, skating over her side, her ribs, and she quivered.

'Cold?' he murmured.

He should get her under the covers, but for the moment he simply wanted to be here…with her. She wrapped her legs around him, pressing herself up into him, and his breath hitched.

'Not around you.'

His hand rose higher, over her bra to the tight knot of her nipple. He circled a finger over it. As his lips plundered hers, Lucy's back arched and she gave a pained moan.

'Like that?' he asked.

'More…'

He smiled as he gazed down at her, Lucy's eyes were glazed and distant as she panted underneath him. 'Greedy.'

But he obliged, happy to feed her desire till she was full with it. His touch was firmer now, like a pinch, and again she arched her body into his palm. He didn't care about himself—not in that moment. All he cared for was Lucy's pleasure, her gasping breaths, the way she quivered under his touch.

He needed to explore all her glorious skin in the warmth of this bed. He moved off her. 'You're wearing too much.'

'So are you.'

Her chest heaved, her gaze glassy and drugged from mere kisses. He couldn't wait to see how she'd look when he'd made love to her for hours.

Stefano wanted to wreck them both.

He hoped the smile he gave her showed his wicked intent. 'I'll come later. For now, this is about *your* pleasure.'

He slid his hands up her body to the top of her leggings, began to drag the fabric down her long legs. She wriggled, trying to help. Made a sound of frustration.

He lifted his hands from her. 'Shh… Be still. Trust me to look after you.'

She stopped moving, lay there quietly with a glorious pout on her lips. 'Hurry.'

He'd prove to her the benefits of going slow.

Little by little the pale expanse of her skin was exposed. He tossed her clothing aside with her socks. Leaned over her with his hands either side of her waist. Dropped his head to touch his lips gently to her belly. Kissed her lower and lower, tracing his tongue over her warm flesh till he reached her underwear.

Then he kissed the heart of her. The scent of her arousal teasing his senses. Driving him on. He hooked his fingers into her panties and tugged them down. Tossed them over his shoulder as his gaze feasted on the curve of her waist, the neat thatch of golden hair between her thighs.

'Open your legs for me.' His voice ground out of him, barely in control.

She did, and he kissed her there. The salt-sweet of her. He closed his eyes and traced his tongue along her overheated flesh. Stroked her inner thighs with his thumbs as she quivered and shook, then speared her hands into his hair and gripped hard. His name on her lips was soft at first, the merest whisper, but it became a chant as he slid a finger into the slick heat of her, then another, and carried her screaming over the precipice.

She lay back, her breaths gulping sobs. The skin under his fingers pebbling with goosebumps. She'd be cold and he was still wearing far too much clothing. He stripped as she watched him, the darkness of her pupils obliterating the gold of her eyes.

'Take off the rest of your clothes.' His voice was all command.

She sat up almost in slow motion, as if moving was too hard, her arms lax and limp. She slipped her top over her head. Unclipped her bra. Her nipples stood tight and high. Stefano's mouth watered. He wanted to give them, and her, the attention they deserved.

Soon.

He thrust his trousers down his legs. Stepped out of them. Kicked them aside, trembling with desire. The need to touch her again drove him on. To make her scream his name once more—louder this time. Because there was no one here who could be witness to the pleasure they shared.

He walked to the side of the bed, drew back the covers. She scrambled under them, her strawberry blonde hair spilling over his pillow as he joined her, gathering her close. She wrapped her arms around him. Traced her roughened fingers over his back, the calluses from years of playing teasing his skin. He thrilled at her touch, at the evidence of her dedication and hard work.

'I need you,' she whispered.

'And you'll have me.'

He rolled over, found protection in his bedside

drawer, sheathed himself. Then he rolled back to Lucy and gathered her softly in his arms. There was no sound in the room other than the panting of their breath and the crackle of the fire. They'd make their own music soon.

He moved over her again. Notched himself at the juncture of her thighs. Took a few breaths to steady himself. He wanted this to last for hours, so both of them could forget. Him, the looming disgrace he'd brought on his family. Lucy, her pain. Her injury. The cheating ex who'd never deserved a woman so precious.

They would each immerse themselves in each other for a while and pretend the real world couldn't touch them. And as he slid inside her he lost himself to the rhythm of their bodies and time ceased to exist.

Lucy's whole life had been all about music. The quest for perfection. Hours when it had felt as if she'd never get anything right. The gruelling travel to another town, another city, when sometimes she hadn't felt settled into any place she could call home.

She'd never thought there was anything else for her and she'd never wanted anything more—till this, and Stefano. His touch was like the music, filling her with the same wondrous heat, like a miracle.

His mouth dropped to hers now, his kisses slick and lush. There was no uncertainty. It was as if they'd been kissing each other for years—as if, for her, there'd been no one before him.

His hands stroked her body with reverence. Setting her on fire. Nothing mattered but the here and now and

Stefano deep inside her body. As if he was connected to her soul in the rightness of how they moved together.

She wrapped her legs around his muscular thighs, the movement of him slow, aching, and every part of her shivered with the perfection of it. Of the time taken to pleasure her. Of the slow, inexorable burn in her core, the sweet ache that wound higher and tighter.

They moved together in perfect tune, as if they were made for one another. Tears pricked at her eyes. The sensation overwhelming her, hovering on the fine edge of pleasure and pain, held there for what felt like hours. She didn't want it to stop, even though she knew things like this couldn't last.

It would all fall down, this house of cards they'd built around themselves. But for however long it lasted, she would take it. She didn't care. For all her life she'd been rooted in reality. Now she wanted to lose herself in the fantasy of them together.

The way he'd looked at her with wonder when she played—not with the critical gaze that everyone else employed, but with one of pure pleasure—was the same way he gazed at her body now, as if she was the most beautiful woman he'd ever glimpsed. And yet she couldn't fall over the edge, still chasing it like some competition to finish.

'More…' she whispered against his lips.

'I want you all afternoon. I want you into the night. And I want to make sure the pleasure lasts and lasts for you, *cara*.'

She couldn't remember anyone who'd only thought of her. She had never really thought about herself— always about work, about practice, about what others

would think. This…her pleasure being his sole focus…
was like a bomb going off inside her. Not a slow burn,
but an explosion that stole her breath, brought raging
heat burning out from her core.

She wrapped herself around him and let it take her,
until he joined her in a rush of ecstasy…

CHAPTER EIGHT

LUCY DRIFTED INTO wakefulness surrounded by delicious warmth. There was a comforting weight over her waist. A hard body spooning her back.

She opened her eyes. The weather outside was gloomy again. But everything inside this room seemed to be bursting with sunshine.

The night before had been…astonishing. She'd only ever had one boyfriend. Her work and her practice had meant that there was little time, and with Viktor their passion had been in the music. It had hardly mattered that the physical side of things hadn't set her on fire.

What a fool she'd been. Stefano was like nothing she could ever have dreamed. The way he'd cared for her, her pleasure, above everything…

That wicked slide of heat began its relentless journey through her again. The need inside urging her to turn in his arms, to kiss him and spend the day in bed, revisiting what they'd shared during the night.

Except she still hadn't said anything about her violin. About the copies of the diary entries she carried. Before, she had been unsure of him. She had no excuses now…

The arm round her waist tightened, and with the merest brush of lips against her neck she forgot all else. She wriggled into Stefano, slick and aching. Felt the press of hardness in her back.

He chuckled. 'I see your passion is not only in your playing.'

'That's not what other people have said.'

Stefano sat up and she turned. The covers had fallen from his body. She relished the hard etched muscles, the strong arms, the hair on his chest arrowing down to the juncture of his thighs. This was a man in his absolute prime and she craved every part of him.

'What fools have said those things about you?'

Viktor. He'd made her practise and practise. He'd always said there was something 'lacking' in her music. Something she needed to find because if she did she might be extraordinary. She'd listened because, whilst he wasn't first violin, he was a brilliant and renowned musician in his own right and she'd thought he had her best interests in mind.

All it had done was make her question her playing. But it felt wrong to mention him now, in this bed, after Stefano had made love to her all night. Had made her forget all her problems and replaced them with only the midnight certainty that she was beautiful and cherished.

Stefano's eyes narrowed. 'It was that ex-boyfriend, wasn't it?'

'He said my playing…"lacked".'

Stefano spat out a string of words which she was sure were profanities from the way he said them, as if they were poison in his mouth.

'Nobody who listens to you could fail to hear the passion in your music. *This* is where I feel it. Right here.'

He took her hand and placed it on his chest, over his heart, which thumped a steady, comforting rhythm under her palm.

'I do think I became lost in my playing…'

'You play like an angel whose heart has been broken and is about to fall. I don't cry, but I wanted to weep at the sound of your music.'

She'd had confidence once, but had begun to feel it was misplaced—slowly chipped away because of her desire to be better, to be perfect, till she'd stopped thinking she could play at all. Once, she'd thought she could achieve anything. When had she begun to believe she was a fraud?

'He was your partner. He should have loved you rather than tried to diminish you. People can be envious of success. He wanted to take yours as his own.'

She looked up at Stefano, so adamant for her when he barely knew her. 'He's acting first violin now in my place.'

'Because of your injury?'

She nodded, the burn of tears stinging her eyes. She wiped them away. Stefano took her hand, began massaging deep into her palm, working his way up her arm. The pleasure of that touch, his care, rippled through her.

'That, and because there were rumours that I'd been saying things about other members of the orchestra… about the conductor. I denied it, but I'm the newest member. The youngest. I didn't tell anyone I was hurting because it almost felt…shameful, how my body had let me down. I hid it from them, thinking I could sort it out myself. It made everyone suspicious about what else I might have hidden. I'm the link between the orchestra and the conductor. I can't do that job if people don't trust me.'

'People are jealous of your talents. That's all.'

'I was told to take some time to think about my future. To try and fix myself. And I don't think they meant physically.'

'There is nothing to fix, *cara*. You're perfect as you are.'

Stefano's touch gentled, became more a stroking, and she moaned. His eyes darkened and the intensity of that gaze was too much. It was as if he saw her in ways that no one else did.

'You are a beautiful, passionate woman and you should not allow *anyone* to try and convince you of otherwise. Your orchestra…? They don't deserve your brilliance.'

The words caught in her chest like a hand grabbing at her heart and twisting. She'd spent her life in a world of competition. A world of music and beauty, sure, but you had to be strong. You didn't always get praise. Most of the time you received criticism. Some of it constructive, a lot of it quite cruel.

Stefano's accolades meant more that he could ever know, and yet she was repaying him by not being honest. The sting of bile rose in her throat. What would he think of her if she were?

'Thank you. But—'

'Accept the praise. You shouldn't qualify it. Don't pay attention to people who try to reduce you to their own mediocrity.'

He picked up her hand and brought her fingertips to

his mouth. Kissed them. The heat of his breath, warm against her flesh. She didn't say anything, just lay there, relishing the attention like a cat being stroked. Her eyes drifted shut as she absorbed the pleasure of it all.

'Okay…'

It was all she could say. His gentle ministrations, his defence of her, had stolen her words and left her only with complicated feelings swirling inside. Soft, warm feelings that she craved to give in to but wouldn't voice.

'I cannot believe that after last night in my bed we're even speaking of another man.' His voice had taken on a deeper tone. Rougher.

She opened her eyes then and he was staring at her, focussed and intent. 'You think you're that good?' she teased.

Stefano raised an eyebrow. The corners of his lips twitched in a smile that wouldn't break free. Yes, he *was* that good—and he knew it. Her body had given her away. Last night had been a revelation of pleasure.

But she didn't want to stroke his ego too much, since he was sitting there looking so assured of his own abilities. Another tease slipped out. 'Or are you jealous?'

'I'm protective of what's mine.'

The force of those words tore through her. *Mine*. She should be outraged that he was so…possessive.

'Oh, I'm yours, am I?'

She'd never truly felt like anyone's before. This sensation—it was fresh. Sharp and bright like the cold fall of snow. And she loved it. A lot too much.

Stefano truly smiled then, and in his smile was something sultry and wicked that told her she would pay, and that he'd enjoy meting out the erotic punishment.

'Should I remind you whose name you called out all night? I owned your pleasure in the early hours. I'll own it again.'

A shiver of desire ran over her, goosebumps peppering her skin. She raised an eyebrow of her own. 'Will you, now?'

'I want you,' he growled, 'and I don't want to be gentle.'

Her breathing came sharp and fast in anticipation of what he might do. 'Then don't be.'

He pounced in a flash. Her hands were pinned lightly above her head under one of his own and his strong, muscular body was covering hers. Lucy's heart beat a wild and uncontrolled rhythm—not out of fear, but with the thrill of being mastered by this man. She opened her legs, his hardness between her thighs. She wanted him inside her so she could forget everything but the pleasure he could bring her.

'Let me see… Where do I start, hmmm…?'

The way the corner of his mouth tipped up in a wicked smirk told her he *knew* what he did to her. The lazy heat running through her veins exploded into something hotter, more potent. She didn't care. She arched her back, trying to get him in the right position, to ease the ache inside that built and built. But the weight of his hips on hers held her down. He could ease up if he wanted to. He was doing it to torment her, make her beg, and she didn't care.

He let go of her hands. 'Don't move them,' he growled.

She froze as he dropped his head, his teeth scraping her nipple. The pleasure of it sizzled through her, arrowing straight between her thighs. She squirmed underneath him. He moved his hips then, sliding over her. She was slick. Wet already. With one change of angle he could be inside her, but he didn't give her enough room.

'Stefano…'

Her voice was a whisper, like a breath of air, and she wondered if he'd heard her. She didn't want to seem as if she was breaking yet. She was trying to extend the pleasure, stretch it out till it snapped with force.

His deep, resonant chuckle was pure wickedness reverberating right through her. And, as much as she needed him, a small, rebellious part of her didn't want to give him the satisfaction of knowing what he did to her. It was a game being played to see who'd succumb first. Except she knew it would be her. Every part of her body strained for him, the pleasure from his touch making her tremble.

'What did you say, *cara*?' He hadn't moved his head far from her left nipple and his breath was warm against her.

'Nothing at all,' she panted.

He took her pebbled nipple into his mouth again. Sucked. Another arrow of pleasure speared between her thighs where he rocked against her. He pulled back again and blew on her, the chill of that stream of air over her damp skin causing her nipple to tighten further. It was hard. Over-sensitive. Too much and not enough all at the same time.

'If you can speak a sentence, I'm not doing a good job.'

If he did any better, she'd die. Right here on the bed. And her reasons for wanting to win this little game be-

came hazy as her body began succumbing to his on-
slaught. To the slide of him as he flexed his hips against
the folds of her, to his attention at her nipple. She held
her hands above her head because it was what he'd de-
manded of her and she hadn't thought to question him.
Her body was completely at the mercy of his.

Another rough scrape of his teeth against her over-
sensitive nipple almost undid her. 'Stefano!'

'Ah, *cara*, are you feeling neglected?'

'*Please*. I—'

'Shh... I'll look after you now.'

He rolled from her and found protection. Then he
was back. Wrapping her in his arms. His kiss was hot,
hard.

'Are you ready for me?'

His voice was pure gravel and it scraped over her in
a shiver of pleasure. He was as affected as her by this
thing between them.

'Yes.'

'Then hold on to me.'

She wrapped her arms around his back as he rose
over her, settled between her thighs and thrust into her.
She almost broke then, at the pleasure and the pain of
him deep inside her as he moved. Hard, just as he'd
warned. Desperate, just as she felt. She clung to him.
Moved with him. Chased her pleasure as he drove into
her. The burn inside her building and building till it
overwhelmed her. Exquisite, electric...

'Say my name.'

His breath was warm against her throat. His voice
all command and she didn't care. She wanted it. Craved

his assertion. He scraped his teeth against the side of her neck and the pleasure rippled through her.

'*Stefano...*'

He groaned. Changed his angle to thrust even deeper. And that was all it took. She was flung over the precipice, soaring into the void with his name once again screaming from her lips.

CHAPTER NINE

STEFANO STRODE THROUGH the castle halls to his room. He'd texted Lucy to meet him there, with instructions to dress for the cold. The weather had cleared, so he'd spent a good part of the afternoon preparing his surprise for her in another of the places here where he'd spent time as a boy.

He didn't know why it was important to show her but, like the conservatory, he thought she would love this too, and her pleasure had become important to him. Vital, like breathing.

When he arrived at his room she was standing outside dressed in her coat and jeans. There was a black and white knitted cap on her head. Fingerless gloves on her hands.

'Cows?' he said, and smiled. 'Do your socks match?'

'Of course.' She held out her hands, showing him that her gloves matched too. 'It wouldn't be me if they didn't.'

'I hope to see them later.'

She raised an eyebrow. 'Only if you're very good.'

Stefano moved close, backed her up against the door. He leaned down and murmured into her ear. 'I was hoping you'd want me to be very…bad.'

He relished the scent of her like a delectable dessert. Lucy gave a pained exhalation. Her hands on his chest, sliding over his shoulders and drawing him close. 'Stefano…'

All he wanted to do was open the door and tumble her into his bed, stay there with her for hours. His willpower was a threadbare thing, but he mustered it nonetheless and stepped away.

He chuckled at her disappointed pout. 'You have the capacity to make me forget everything I'm meant to be doing. But I have something to show you and I won't be swayed.'

'You're being enigmatic.'

He'd wanted her trust, and yet he knew that after what she had been through with the betrayal by her ex it would have to be earned.

'You asked about my favourite places here. I've another to show you—somewhere I particularly enjoyed in my early teens. It's a surprise.'

He began to walk and she followed. Her smile was bright and happy. The look on her face could chase away all the cold in this place.

'Did you spend much time in the castle when you were younger?' she asked.

'Until I was in the equivalent of your high school, yes. We lived here with whichever nanny and specialist tutors my parents had employed, whilst they were in the city during the social season and for work.'

Her eyebrows raised. 'So you were left alone?'

'My parents subcontracted their responsibilities. Their main aim was to ensure we didn't disgrace ourselves, but once the future of the Moretti name was assured by my birth, and then that of my brother, they felt they'd done their duty. Their role was to maintain their status as one of Lasserno's premier families, which had always been their main interest.'

'What about you?'

Stefano shrugged. 'There are many things children can do when the eyes on them aren't as watchful as they should be. It wasn't all bad. Given that my role as the future Count of Varno was assured, I had no real concerns. I watched out for my siblings. I was in charge of them in many ways.'

'That sounds…lonely.' Lucy frowned. 'What about friends?'

He shrugged. Sometimes he'd missed the company of children his own age, but occasionally the staff here would bring their children to the castle, for him and his siblings to play with. His parents would have been horrified, so no one had ever told them.

'Alessio's was the only friendship that was really encouraged.'

Lucy placed her hand on his arm as they walked. 'That's sad. You realise, don't you?'

Her sympathy, her support, almost stopped him. She could never understand how much it meant against the pain from that time, of almost losing his sister and being forced to accept responsibility too young. Not being encouraged to mix with others like a normal boy. He hadn't recognised back then how it had shaped his life.

'Perhaps—if we hadn't liked each other. Luckily, we did. He became like another brother to me.'

It was as if a hand had plunged into his chest, tear-ing out his heart at that acknowledgement. The loss of Alessio's friendship was a wound that would likely never heal. But there was so little he could tell her. He didn't want this moment ruined by the admission of his failings, but there was so much he wanted to say.

'Since I've been back taking care of the castle's repairs it's the first time in years we haven't worked together in some way. That's been…challenging. It has always been my role to assist him in whichever way was best.'

It wasn't exactly the truth, but it gave voice to a small part of his reality.

Lucy frowned. 'I can't imagine that kind of expectation.'

'What about you?' he asked. 'Did you always know you wanted to play the violin, or was it something imposed upon you by your parents because of your mother's talent?'

'How did you—?'

'Internet.'

He smiled, trying to recover from the error of that admission. He knew far more about Lucy than she'd disclosed to him. He should probe her about the coronation ring now. In his not doing so there was a lack of truth between them which needled his conscience. But now was not the moment. He intended to put another of those blazing smiles on her face. And whilst they were snowed in, there was still time…

'You have a history. Some might say you're living up to it.'

'My mother encouraged me, and from the moment I saw her playing it was what I wanted to do. I never questioned it until recently, but now I'm wondering who I am if I can't play.'

It seemed they were both questioning their place in the world.

Celine's words inched into his consciousness again. *'Who are you...?'* He shut them down.

They'd moved into some of the lesser-used service corridors. Places he'd played in as a child, creating fantasies of knights and of dragons he and his siblings were required to slay. As children, they'd always been victorious. It was only as an adult that he'd come to realise that life didn't always work out the way you thought it would.

He glanced over at Lucy again. He'd like to slay *her* dragons. She didn't deserve the treatment that had been meted out to her, causing her to question her playing, her talents.

'Where on earth are you taking me?' she asked.

'You'll have to wait and see. Ah, here we are.'

They'd arrived at a wooden door made of rough-hewn slabs of wood and hand-forged cast iron hinges. He'd unlocked it earlier, when he'd come to make the space ready for her.

Stefano tugged at the handle and the door creaked open to reveal a dimly lit stone staircase.

'How many steps are there?' she asked.

'I've never counted them—but, trust me, the effort is worth it.'

He'd set up his own space here as a teenager, for those times when his siblings had become too much and he'd wanted a place to be alone. It had given him perspective. A reminder that there were things bigger than himself, and that his problems were small compared to the vastness of the universe before him. He'd studied here, dreamed here of a life and a future that he'd thought would be grand and important. Of how he might be better than all the Counts before him, stamping his indelible mark on the role.

How naïve he'd been. Those dreams all seemed so futile now. He'd marked the role with a blot of ink so black and dark it might never wash clean.

They'd reached the top of the stairs and Lucy waited whilst he opened another ancient door into the room he'd readied for her. He'd never brought anyone here before. It was the one place in the castle he'd kept all to himself. Not even Celine had seen this place...his teenage sanctuary. She wouldn't have been impressed, given it lacked the grandeur of the rest of the castle.

What would Lucy think of it?

He wasn't sure why the answer to that question was so important.

He turned on the torch, then took Lucy's hand and led her through, closing the door on the dimly lit stairwell behind them. At least the room was a bit warmer than freezing, with the space heater he'd placed in the corner working hard to heat the area. It was a difficult task since there was so much glass around them.

He moved to the edge of the room, out of the way of the furniture, and turned off the torch again.

Lucy's fingers squeezed his. 'Where are we and why are the lights out?' she whispered.

'We're in the eastern turret. Let your eyes adjust.'

In days long past the room had been encased by windows, rather than leaving it open, and it was the perfect place to view the province his family had supported over centuries. Tonight there was little light outside, the moon a bare sliver, which was perfect for what he had in mind. The only sounds were their breathing and the gentle brush of a cold breeze.

He tugged on her hand. 'This leads to the ramparts. I hope you're not afraid of heights.'

There was no risk of falling, the walls were higher than his own waist, but they were a long way above ground. Still, it wasn't looking down that he was interested in.

'I'm not afraid if I'm with you.'

Lucy's words struck at the very heart of him. In those moments he believed that he was once again a man of honour, of worth. She followed him with no hesitation.

He stepped out first to test the temperature, and the frigid air hit him like a slap. Lucy wouldn't like it, but he hoped what he had to show her would compensate for the cold weather she loathed.

'It's freezing,' she said, her breath like puffs of smoke in the night air.

'I know, but we won't be here for long and I'll keep you warm.' He stood behind her and wrapped his arms round her body, barely able to feel her under the downy coat she wore. 'Look up.'

Her head moved back against his chest. 'Oh. *Wow*.'

He looked up himself, and saw the clear black night sky was peppered with thousands of stars. The wonder of it caught him the same way it had when he'd first seen this as a boy, climbing into the forbidden tower and realising that the world was a far bigger place than just him and his family. The perspective had been a humbling one.

'You wanted to see stars.' He tightened his arms round her and rested his chin on the top of her head. 'Whilst these aren't the stars you see from your home, I hope they're enough.'

'This is so special. What an amazing place…' She turned in his arms. The slender moon's glow washed over her face, pale and ghost-like in the silvery light. 'Thank you.'

'It's my pleasure to share this with you.' It meant everything to hear the wonder in her voice. To see how she appreciated his retreat, its beauty. 'I've never brought anyone here before.'

She had given him her music, and he had nothing to give in return other than what he could show her. The conservatory…this secret place. The areas of his home most special to him…

He'd given her a key to parts of his life few had been allowed to glimpse. And in doing so, it was terrifying for him to feel how *right* this moment seemed, when everything else in his life was wrong. She'd given him that without realising, and he didn't know how to thank her without divulging all his sins. He didn't want her thinking less of him. Better for tonight to live in the delusion that things between them could stay just as they were.

Silhouetted against the glimmering lights of the city in the distance, Lucy tilted her head back again. There was the merest of sparkle in her eyes as whatever light was available caught there and glittered.

'I've missed seeing the stars.'

He cupped her face in his hands, his thumbs sliding over the soft skin, slick in areas with what felt suspiciously like tears.

'It's so beautiful…'

There was a sound to her voice, a crack in it. As if it was broken with emotion. It cracked something inside him, too. Stefano was almost certain her tears were happy ones, but he didn't want her to cry. He wanted to bring her joy. The need for that overwhelmed him—the need to comfort, protect. To make her…*happy*.

'Lucy…'

He dropped his mouth to hers, found her lips warm and soft under his own. Parting, letting him in. And once again he was lost.

Lucy tightened her arms round Stefano's waist. Her bulky jacket, her gloves, were an interruption to the feel of his body against hers. Still, the heat of him rushed through her like a burst of hot water. She couldn't get enough of him. He seemed like such a hard, uncompromising man, but his kisses…they were all gentleness.

This was beyond what she'd already experienced, the passion. There was something more. He'd trusted her with this special place, which he'd never shown another. It all overwhelmed her, like her music, and she was lost in him, trembling in his arms again.

His kiss slowed, stopped. His heavy, warm breaths gusted for a moment against her cheeks. He pulled away and she wanted to shout *No!* To drag him back to a place where they could both get lost in each other. Forget everything but the magic they made together.

'Come inside. You should get warm. With all the

windows, you can still see the stars. It's freezing out here.'

He took her hand, laced his fingers through her own and walked her inside. The room seemed quite cosy, considering they were in a turret, and it was frigid outside, but she couldn't get a good view of the space in the darkness. She'd only caught glimpses of it in the torchlight.

Stefano unthreaded his fingers from hers, left her standing in the centre of the room. Even through her soles of her boots the floor seemed softer here. A rug, perhaps? There was a striking sound, a hiss, and the glimmer of light from a match as he lit something. A candle. Then another. And another. Stefano went through three matches before a golden light glowed in the room. Then he walked towards her, guided her to a plump couch where she sat down.

She could see it now, the small square space. A single bed, a desk... The bulk of the floor was covered in a plush rug, as she'd guessed, and the rest was polished stone.

'Here's a blanket.'

He handed her the heavy, silky-soft fabric and she wrapped it around her knees. Then he reached for a vacuum flask and unscrewed the lid. He poured out a cup of something and the scent of chocolate teased her nose.

He handed it to her. 'This will help.'

'Thank you.' She took a long sip of sweet, perfect hot chocolate. 'It's not as cold in here as outside.'

'I turned on a heater, but it's not the most efficient way of warming the space. This place was meant for protecting the castle. I'm sure my ancestors didn't want the people guarding it to get too comfortable.'

'It looks like it's been made comfortable.'

This would have taken time and effort. The candles, the heater, the drink... Walking up and down that flight of stairs multiple times, because it likely would have taken more than one trip. He'd thought about this. He'd done it for her.

The burn of tears teased at her eyes again. This man—he was all risk. And she was deceiving him by not telling him about the violin, by allowing herself to be lost in this world that they inhabited together rather than ruining precious moments like this, in a fantasy place where everything going on outside the castle didn't matter.

But for now she'd relish the time with him. This big, beautiful grand gesture from a man who would likely not admit to any softness.

She blinked the errant tears away. Settled back into the cushions as he sat beside her. 'What is this place used for now?'

He looked around the room and an expression crossed his face. Something almost wistful. 'Not for anything. I keep it furnished for sentimental reasons. It was my escape when I was younger. Being in charge of the castle and my siblings when I was only a teenager was difficult at times. At my request, the staff took some furniture from the lesser-used rooms and made this place for me.'

'It must have been hard, being so responsible.'

He sat staring at the candles on a small table, his eyes unfocussed. 'It wasn't all responsibility. We ran wild much of the time. I was their leader. For the most part we had fun.'

'For the most part?'

'Children aren't easy to look after, and my younger siblings felt neglected by me at times, I'm sure. They certainly felt neglected by my parents. One evening my younger sister decided she wanted to see my mother, who'd worn a grand ball gown to go to the capital. Emilia packed a bag and left the castle. It was winter. We were lucky that dinner was early that night or we'd never have noticed her missing. Even luckier that fresh snow had fallen and we could follow her footprints, or we would have lost her. From that day on, I never forgot my responsibility to my siblings. To keep them safe. To protect them.'

Lucy reached out and laid her hand over Stefano's for comfort. His skin was warm under her fingers. 'At least they're adults now.'

'I'll always be responsible for them. Lasserno can be unforgiving—especially for my siblings. Social climbing is an aristocratic sport here, and my brother and sister aren't interested in playing that competitive game. I had the protection of the Crown, but they wanted something different from life... What I do has an impact on them and always will.'

Stefano was so responsible. He was looking after *her*. She wished she could look after him for a change. He desperately needed someone to give him a little softness in his life.

'Thank you for showing me this place. Your home is beautiful. You must miss it when you're not here.'

'I've been neglecting it. Celine didn't like the castle, or the mountains. The things she used to say about them...' He laughed, but it was a bitter sound with no pleasure in it. 'So I stayed away when I should have been here. My brother cares for the conservatory but that's all he's really interested in. My sister is busy studying. The responsibility for this place is mine and I've failed it. You're suffering the consequences.'

'I'm getting used to the temperature.'

'You shouldn't have to.' He took her hands between his and the heat of them slid through her fingers. 'Are you cold now?'

'Never around you.' It was as simple and as complicated as that. He might be dark and brooding, and there was something around him that wasn't entirely happy, but Stefano carried the heat of sunlight. It was a truth she could admit when other things between them were a lie.

She wished she could talk to him, tell him what she needed to before her secrets eroded everything beautiful between them, but she couldn't find the right words. Not here in this space together, cocooned against the world, where she could kid herself with the fantasy that reality couldn't touch them. She'd allowed a sense of inevitability to overtake her. As if there was nowhere else they should be.

She didn't know who moved first—her or him—but somehow they were closer and their lips touched again. She opened underneath him. His mouth was a gentle tease against her own and all she craved was more, *deeper*. She could forget when his lips were on hers, when his arms were banding her body, when he was inside her. Her worries dissolved and her pain disappeared with the pure and perfect need. Nothing mattered. Not the orchestra. Not her violin. There was her, and him, and it was enough.

Her hands skated around the waist of his hard body, tugged at the warmth of his sweater. She slipped them under his shirt to stroke his hot skin and he flinched away, a smile on his lips.

'You say you're not cold, but your fingers are.'

'Then keep me warm.'

Stefano moaned and took her in his arms. His lips crashed onto hers in a move that took rather than gave. She didn't care. She wanted to forget again, and she would give everything in this moment for their bodies to be skin to skin, with his hard, muscular frame covering hers.

His sure hands unzipped her coat, pushed it from her shoulders. The cool air of the room held a sting, but it was nothing when compared to the passion and heat that they generated together. He broke from the kiss and stood, holding out his hands to her. She placed her chilled ones into his and he helped her stand. He walked them to the narrow bed and drew back the covers, then hesitated.

'I'm sorry…perhaps we should go somewhere else.'

Lucy looked up into his black eyes, gleaming in the candlelight. She cupped his cheek and the stubble teased her palm. 'No, here's perfect.'

'Good. I'm not sure that I can wait.'

He undid the button of her jeans, slid down the zip and eased them from her hips, down her thighs, as his hands skimmed her legs. He crouched on his knees before her and pressed his hot lips to her belly, then lower, his warm breaths gusting over her skin.

'You are so beautiful…' he murmured against her flesh as he kissed her at the juncture of his thighs. Moving her underwear aside, he let his tongue explore, gently toying with her, and she was frozen in pleasure till he stopped. The only sound in the room was her panting breaths.

He helped her out of her boots, her jeans. 'On the bed,' he said, his voice dark and rough.

She trembled at the need his words exposed, at the fact that she'd done this—moved such an implacable man. She lay down, the sheets cold and crisp underneath her.

Stefano shucked his own trousers, the rest of his clothes, till he stood perfect, naked and erect, in the soft glow of candlelight. The illumination etched the shadows of his muscles deeper, made them magnificently defined. She lay back, glorying in the masculine perfection of his hard, male body, admiring the work and dedication he must put into it. Into everything.

His dedication and attention now being directed towards her.

He joined her on the bed and pulled the sheets and thick down cover over them both. His hands skated under her top to stroke her skin and she shivered at the pleasure of his touch. A sweet ache built deep inside her.

Stefano unclipped her bra and his hand reached for her breast, stroking her nipple till it beaded. The sensation stung like an electric shock through her, between her legs. His muscular body was against hers, the crisp hair on his legs teasing her skin. His head dropped to her nipple, his tongue smooth and insistent as her flesh responded to his ministrations, her hands clawing into his back.

Stefano chuckled, then the sound was cut off as he wrapped his lips round her nipple and sucked, slipping a hand between her thighs. She was close. This man set her aflame. She might have once thought music was her only passion, that playing the violin was everything to her, but Stefano Moretti was fast turning into a dangerous obsession.

She shook under his ministrations, not wanting to tip over the glorious edge without him. 'I need you…'

'You have me,' he murmured against her skin, and a rush of heat coursed inside her at the desire that once again roughened his voice. But he didn't stop his insistent stroking of her overheated flesh.

'Inside me.'

All of him stilled. 'Whatever you want that is in my power to give you, Lucy, I will.'

His touch and his body might inflame her, but those words… They spoke of more than sex or infatuation. More than passion. They speared right to the heart of her, and she couldn't think or even dream of what they might mean.

She held a secret, and now it almost felt like a betrayal not to tell him. Some might say it didn't matter—that the violin had been in her family for over seventy-five years and why should she care where it had come from after all that time?

But to her honesty was everything. She'd seen how her father's lack of it had eaten away and destroyed things. How Viktor's cowardice had meant his having an affair rather than confronting the failure of their relationship. She always wanted the truth, even if it was brutal and hurt her, left her bleeding. Better that than living in blissful ignorance only to have life as you knew it pulled away from you at the last minute.

'Where did you go?'

Stefano's words dragged her out of those dark thoughts. She should say something, but his hands were stroking her again, drifting over her skin, and all she craved was to shut her eyes and give in to the sensation.

She reached up to his face and drew her thumb across his lips, gazed into his meltingly dark eyes that gleamed with flickers of gold in the light. 'I'm right here.'

'If you're still coherent, I'm not doing my job.' He grasped her top and bra and took them off in one go, tossing them on the floor. 'That's better. Now there's nothing between us.'

But there was. He deserved more than this. But she didn't know what to say when all she wanted was to lose herself in him again. 'Please, Stefano.'

He reached down to his trousers on the floor. Grabbed protection. Sheathed himself, then settled over her.

'You came prepared.' She parted her legs, gloried in the feel of him notched between her thighs. Awaiting the pleasure that was so close, everything to come.

'I always want you. It's like an obsession.'

In that way their feelings were terrifyingly mutual, but there was something else which screamed of a desire for much more. Permanence.

Stefano dropped his mouth to hers, his kiss slick, hard and intent. As their tongues touched and she wrapped her arms tight around his body once more he slid into her. Her back arched at the pleasure of him deep inside her body. She was so close, even now. This man inflamed her, set her alight.

He moved and their bodies melded, the beautiful song of their lovemaking echoing round them in the small, intimate space. Lucy tightened her arms around his torso. Wrapped her legs round him. Glorying in the feel of his hard body against hers.

The way they moved together was pure instinct and an innate knowledge of each other's desires. She didn't want this night to end. That need chanted in her head as her body tightened, climbing higher and higher. The burn building inside her. Waiting for the brilliant snap of pleasure that he held just out of reach.

He murmured words—some in English, some in Italian. Gentle things about her beauty, words of encouragement, telling her how much pleasure she gave him. None of them pushed her off the delicious edge she walked, held in an endless fog of pleasure. Then there were more whispered words, ones she wasn't sure he'd want her to hear, lost as they both were in the moment together.

'How will I get enough of you?'

They were like a match to kindling. She burned with the ferocity of petrol flung at a fire. An explosion of pleasure she wasn't sure she'd survive as the sensation burst inside her, rending her in two, and she sobbed his name to the stars.

CHAPTER TEN

LUCY LOOKED OUT of the window of the music room, where she'd decided to play—perhaps one of her last chances to do so. The snow had stopped. There was little question that the roads were passable and there was now no excuse for her to stay. Except she didn't want to go.

She'd moved from thinking she could never allow herself to be vulnerable with a man again to sharing some of her deepest fears and dreams with Stefano. The thought of leaving him stung like an open wound in the sea. So she took the pain and did what she had always done with it.

She played.

The piece was a simple one, but something she loved. The perfect acoustics of the room amplified the tune. Sweet and gentle. Almost hopeful. It was how she felt—about her playing, at least.

Without the pressure of performance there wasn't any stiffness or pain in her hands. Her fears over her injury had lessened, and she'd begun to love the music again. It was what she'd missed. Not learning something complicated to thrill a crowd, or a piece she didn't enjoy because that was what her performance schedule required. There was no need to strive, because she was enough. Lucy knew now that she wasn't a fraud. You didn't get to the position of first violin by fooling anyone. You either had the ability or you didn't.

Stefano had given that back to her. Restored the confidence that had been slowly yet relentlessly eroded till she'd questioned everything. She allowed herself to see her musicianship through his eyes. Remembered the wonder on his face as he'd watched her play. It was a feeling she allowed to be mirrored inside herself, because he believed in her abilities. Believed in *her*.

And she'd begun believing in herself again too. Cocooned here in this place, it was as if her creative well had been refilled, with passion blossoming. Somewhere along the way something had happened to her with this brooding, complicated man. A man she didn't want to leave.

She still hadn't been honest with him about her violin. In the beginning she'd been scared to say anything till she had the measure of him. Now…? Now she had no excuse other than the realisation that telling him would change everything. The guilt of keeping her secret after the care he'd shown, after they'd made love, was a brutal voice that whispered in her ear about how she'd failed him.

She was sure he'd think that too, the moment she said something. There was no excuse for leaving it so long other than her selfish desire not to change this fragile, beautiful thing between them. To pretend that the outside world didn't exist, protected as they were by the winter around them. But reality always intruded.

She finished her piece, loosened the strings of her bow, and packed her beloved violin back into its case. Her parents' lawyers were still arguing over whether it formed part of the marital property pool, but it didn't matter. She'd come to realise that even in wartime you didn't hand such a valuable possession to a stranger without it involving some obligation.

Her grandfather had carried that obligation and his sense of guilt till he died. His carefully written diaries hinted at the weight of it—how it had almost crushed him some days. His final words in those last weeks, whilst confused, had spoken of a loss and guilt that plagued him. Of taking something that wasn't his, to save himself when everything else around him was lost.

It was time for her to complete the mission he'd started over seventy-five years ago. Time to set his memory free.

The door cracked open and her heart began to thump in an excited kind of rhythm. It was like the anticipation of waiting in the wings backstage, just before walking on to perform.

Stefano came into the room and shut the door behind him. She wasn't sure she would ever get enough of this man. In her quieter moments Lucy realised that she wanted to make her reality here, if only she could ignore her fears of bursting the shimmering bubble of possibility that surrounded them.

She smiled, but that smile rapidly faded. An energy she couldn't place crackled round him like static. His eyes were dark and glittering as he stared at her with an intensity that caused a shiver to race over her spine. Something was wrong. She knew it. Could feel it intuitively. It was like the sound of a violin when its strings were over-tight. Everything about him was discordant. Too sharp.

'You seem…tense. Everything okay?'

Stefano's hands clenched, released. He flexed his fingers. 'I took a phone call assuming it was you, so I didn't check the number before answering.'

His voice cut her, sharp and cold, like the whistle of the wind in the ramparts of this place.

'Instead, I was forced into conversation with His Highness's private secretary.'

'I thought *you* were His Highness's private secretary and you were just here repairing the castle?'

Pain was etched on every part of him—in the tense set of his shoulders, the tightness around his eyes, the brutal slash of his mouth.

'Don't believe everything you read or hear.'

Lucy walked up to him, reached out and placed her hand on his chest. The heat of him reassured her, when he otherwise appeared wrapped in cold and darkness. The moment seemed fragile and hesitant, and then Stefano dropped his head, took a step back and away from her. It might have been only centimetres, but it felt like an uncrossable chasm.

'Stefano, who hurt you?'

If she hadn't been staring at his face, searching for the answer, she might have missed it. But there was a flinch, as if he'd been waiting for a strike.

'Some of the deepest wounds are self-inflicted.'

Each word sounded as if it had been ground through glass, shredding him as it was spoken.

'Recently I've come to think most things can be

fixed,' she said. He'd allowed her to believe that—one of the many gifts he'd given her in her brief time here.

Stefano gave a short, sharp laugh, more mocking than amused. 'I wish I had your naïvety. Some mistakes can't be repaired.'

Time for her to discuss her own error—not talking to him earlier about the violin and what she knew. She needed to leap into the void and trust that it would work out, because somewhere in her time here she'd begun trusting him. First with her safety, with her body, and then with her heart. It terrified her, because there was only guessing and hope. But she realised now what she'd tried to ignore: this endless warmth suffusing her, the catch and thrum of her heart every time he came near, the emotions she'd refused to give voice to, could only mean one thing.

She loved him.

And she wanted him to love her back.

Maybe she was naïve, as he'd accused her of being, but the future she hoped for could only happen if there was truth between them. She couldn't go back to the beginning, so they'd have to start again today. She'd found the courage to do so now she believed in herself, and more importantly in him. Because she'd come to understand one thing in the time she'd been here. In a world of men who'd let her down—her father, her exboyfriend, and in a way her grandfather, with all his human failings—there was still a man who'd proved he could be honourable.

This man who'd shown her the stars.

'You're a good person, Stefano.'

His eyes narrowed. His look was piercing and hard,

as if he was assessing her worth and somehow finding her lacking. 'Would you forgive a man who betrayed you?'

Betrayal she knew all about.

She wrapped her arms around her waist. He could be talking about Viktor, but she was sure there was more than one meaning in everything Stefano was saying right now. A riddle she was being forced to solve.

What else could he mean? He'd said he no longer had a fiancée—maybe he'd lied about that? Nausea churned in her stomach, as if she'd taken a hefty swallow of sour milk. What did she really know of him, anyhow? She'd only been here a week, and he'd promised her nothing.

No. He'd promised her she was welcome. He promised she'd be safe. He'd given her both of those things. Whilst she hadn't much trusted her instincts over the past months, she didn't believe his sincerity had been faked.

'I *know* you. You're not like Viktor.'

'Not in deed, but in every other way I'm the same. You say you know me…' He stabbed his fingers at the middle of his chest, as if punctuating every word on his flesh. 'Maybe I should tell you who I really am in the spirit of honesty. Honesty between people is important, isn't it?'

He turned his back on her and stalked to the window, and as he did so she caught a glimpse of his expression. Lip curled in a sneer, dark and ugly. But she didn't think it was directed at her, given he was now staring into the melting landscape outside, towards the capital. It was as if he *loathed* himself.

She shook her head. 'You're the man who took me in.

Gave me his bed. Showed me his home. You're some-one who's kind, considerate—'

He whipped round. Took a few steps towards her. Stopped. 'I resigned my position as the Prince's private secretary after betraying him. My best friend. Report-ing his private movements to the press. I brought dis-honour and disrepute to my family.'

She didn't know what to say. Her voice had been stolen by his revelation. He'd been pretending he still had the role all the time she'd been here. How could he have done something like that? They'd talked of it— the responsibility, the obligation—and it wasn't a job he held at all. What had he been doing when he'd claimed to be working, locked in his office during the day, and on some evenings well into the night?

Lucy swallowed down the knot in her throat. Tried to dig up the trust in Stefano she'd found over the time she'd been here rather than turning away and leaving. And whilst the voice of warning in her head whis-pered that he was a liar and didn't care about her, she saw that Stefano wasn't standing before her uncaring. He'd dropped his head. His shoulders rose and fell as if the weight he carried would soon crush him. It was as though he'd taken a fatal wound and was about to bleed out on the floor.

Lucy knew that nothing would help this type of in-jury, because it looked as if it had damaged Stefano's soul. Bad people didn't give a damn about that kind of wound. Guilt was only suffered by those who had a conscience, who knew right from wrong and regretted their actions and the hurt they'd caused to others. That knowledge was all she needed to keep her in the room.

'Why did you do it?' she asked. 'Because intention is everything.'

'My reasons may have been sound, but the "why" is irrelevant. I have a meeting at the palace in one week. It's not enough time for me to finish the work I've started. You have kept me from it. Distracted me in *every* way. And now my time's run out.'

He looked at her then, and his eyes were narrowed. Cold, like black ice chips.

'You have something I want.'

Dread flowed over her like a shower of iced water. He'd told her nothing whilst she was here other than he'd been looking for jewels. Stefano couldn't know about the violin, could he?

Lucy took some long, slow breaths, as if preparing herself for a performance, and in many ways she was. The performance of her life. The future rested on what she was about to say.

'I think you're right. That's what I need to talk to you about. The real reason I'm here.'

For a few precious moments Stefano had hoped that Lucy would have no idea what he was talking about, no knowledge of the past that had entwined their families and cursed him. Her words ended that lingering fantasy.

She'd stayed here with the knowledge all along. Eating his food, sleeping in his bed, sleeping with *him*—and for what? She was just another woman using him for her own agenda, like Celine. But what did it matter when his life was now on a collision course with Alessio?

The message had been polite, yet firm and clear. The

meeting was non-negotiable. Letters could be ignored, as he'd successfully done over the past few months. A personal demand could not.

The words of Alessio's new private secretary still buzzed in his ears like violent white noise. There had been mention of Stefano's role as patron of the orchestra, and an important but undisclosed personal request. Now he could barely contain the heat inside him, which reached volcanic levels as he battled the tide that threatened to burst free. The anger at himself for his failure, for allowing Lucy to distract him.

This was his last moment to make things right for his siblings. Whatever the cost, he would not fail them again.

He walked towards Lucy. She looked up at him, her golden eyes wide, her teeth worrying her bottom lip.

'In the dying days of the Second World War, as the enemy approached to occupy this castle, my family gave Lasserno's coronation ring to an Australian soldier with links to the underground movement, to take to safety.'

'Wait...what?'

A frown creased her brow. She appeared confused. But there was no confusing what he'd said. The facts were incontrovertible.

'I don't know anything about a ring. I only know about my violin.'

It was a delightful and compelling act—but then Celine had fooled him for five years, professing love and adoration when it had all been lies. It simply proved how easily he fell for a beautiful face. A willing body.

'I am not interested in some fiddle.'

'It's no *fiddle*—and there's no ring...only the violin

and what my grandfather's diaries say. Something about it being Lasserno's heart.'

Stefano's own heart stuttered, missed a beat. Those words alone were enough to confirm what he knew. But to have *diaries* as evidence?

'Another name for the coronation ring was the Heart of Lasserno, after its flawless central ruby. How could your grandfather talk about Lasserno's heart if he didn't have the ring? It's no coincidence.'

His words were hissed through clenched teeth as he began to pace, trying to hold back his frustration at her equivocation when *everything* rode on this.

'And yet my investigations show that your family has no great riches. It's unremarkable except for your father's parlous financial history.'

Lucy rocked back, a hand to her chest. 'You had me investigated?'

In a moment of weakness Stefano hesitated, almost reached out to steady her, to take her in his arms and whisper that everything would be okay. But *nothing* here was okay.

'Exactly how long have you suspected that my family had something valuable of yours?' she asked.

'When you mentioned your grandfather's name. Arthur Hunter. "Art", you called him. My family archives talk of a man—Art Cacciatore. Despite extensive searches I could never find him, but *cacciatore* means "hunter" in Italian. Something else that's no coincidence.'

The colour ran high on her cheeks. Two ruddy red strips on her otherwise pale skin.

'You knew from the beginning. All this time.'

She shook her head, almost as if disappointed. As if he was yet another person to add to a growing list. But she was no innocent in this twisted tale. Her feelings didn't matter here—only his brother and sister did.

'Where is the ring, Lucy?'

She threw up her hands. 'I keep trying to tell you. There's only the violin. My grandfather's diary mentions someone telling him to save himself, and he says that Lasserno's heart saved him. You say it's a ring, but the violin saved him. I've told you this story. In his last days he seemed crippled by guilt over it all.'

What did he care for the violin? He'd not completed the task he'd set out to achieve. There would be no glorious homecoming for his nation's treasure. His quest for redemption had come to an ignominious end.

Stefano shoulders slumped, and exhaustion threatened to cut him down at the knees. How would he free his brother and sister now?

'That coronation ring was priceless...'

Lucy took a step forward, looked into his face, faltered. She stepped back. 'So is the violin. I was told my whole life that it was one of many valuable reproductions, but when my grandfather died and we found his diaries we discovered that it was real. A Stradivarius.' She pointed, jabbing her finger at the case where it now sat, on top of the grand piano. 'Up until now it's been thought that all the existing Strads are known. A new one will create history—a storm in the music world. My grandfather talked of the violin being Lasserno's heart and Lasserno's heart saving him. What if...? I don't know...'

Lucy began to pace, clenching and unclenching her

hands. 'What if they're one and the same? Maybe he swapped the ring for the violin whilst on the run? To keep himself alive? A jewel couldn't help him, but a violin could. Maybe he saw the Stradivarius as fair trade, because he knew the value of what he was being given? Swapping one priceless object for another. It's all a guess, but I can't be sorry about it. Because without the violin I might not be here.'

Sorry... It was a mere word. It wasn't enough. She'd travelled to Lasserno for this reason and stayed silent.

'You came to my home with that knowledge and you did not say *anything* to me.'

Lucy reached out her hands, as if imploring him to engage his softer feelings. Her entreaty was wasted. Any remaining softness inside him had suffered its final death throes.

'You knew as well—maybe not about the violin, but about my grandfather. We've both been hiding from this, Stefano. But I was always going to say something. My grandfather *loved* Lasserno. He talked endlessly about it. I said to you before that I believe he left a part of himself here. I genuinely came here to...to learn about you and your family.'

Her words were pretty, but they didn't change the truth. 'One thing is clear. You didn't find me worthy enough to tell the story.'

'That's not what I said. And if you believed my family had the coronation ring why didn't you say anything to me?'

He gritted his teeth, fighting the bile that rose in his throat. 'There's an Italian saying: *To trust is good; not to trust is better.* It's now my motto to live by. I would *never* trust the words of someone like you, whose relative stole from my family. My country. Who didn't say anything until she was caught out.'

All this time Lucy had looked as if she was ready for a fight. She had been standing tall and proud, almost regal in her demeanour—and he knew royalty. But after those words it was as if she was a tree, felled by the fatal blow of an axe. There was a desperate final teeter and then she seemed to topple.

'And I thought I'd fallen...' Her voice hitched. Her mouth was downcast, her gaze hollow and blank, her eyes glistening. 'We...we made love and you didn't trust me at all.'

'What we did had *nothing* to do with love.'

The lesson was a painful one, but it was one she should learn. All her talk of him being a good man... She couldn't have meant any of it. Because if she'd truly believed he was good she would have said something to him before he'd confronted her. Well, he'd show Lucy now. Her faith in him was utterly misguided. There was no good left in him.

'And now you learn the man I truly am, *cara*. You know it all.'

'You're right. Trusting someone's good intentions hurts too much. Not trusting is *much* better.' She dropped her head. Scuffed at the floor with her booted foot. All the brightness in her had died, like a candle snuffed out. 'Now the snow's gone I assume Bruno can reach the castle? I'll call him and leave.'

She turned. Began walking to the door. Stopped. Her shoulders rose and fell but she still faced away from him, as if she couldn't bear to look at him ever again.

'My grandfather always said the violin saved his life. Recently, to me, it's felt like an impossible burden. For you, Stefano… I hope it sets you free.'

Stefano sat outside Alessio's office in the palace visitors' area. He'd never thought he'd be waiting like a stranger when this place had once been so familiar to him it had been a second home. He hadn't wanted to walk through these doors again until his self-appointed work was complete. The call had come too early. He only hoped he'd done enough, since he hadn't retrieved all the Crown Jewels yet. And as for the coronation ring…

Distraction had come into his life, taken him away from what he had to do. An arrow of pain shot through him. He wouldn't think of that distraction now. He wouldn't think of *her*. He tried to shut down the visions tripping through his mind of sunshine, of strawberry blonde hair. Of freedom and allowing himself to dream rather than settling himself into cold reality.

The cold was where he belonged.

In his hands he held what he hoped would be his family's redemption. That was all that mattered. His brother and sister would be free. They would leave Lasserno, and be able to escape any misplaced censure for his personal failings. It was what he wanted for them. His own future was meaningless now. He'd held a glimmering possibility in his hands for the briefest of moments, shining brighter than the gemstones he'd recovered, till he'd rejected it all.

He would never forget the lines of hurt etched on her beautiful face as he'd said what he had.

Lucy.

He gasped against the pain, like a soul torn in two. It was nothing. *She* was nothing. She couldn't be. Who would want someone like him? He simply wouldn't think about her.

Yet as Stefano placed the precious violin case on the ground, he almost doubled over with the agony of it all.

The ornate door in front of him cracked open. It was time, but his ruined heart barely changed its rhythm. He wasn't sure it knew how to beat. It was as cold and dead as it had been when Lucy had first walked into his home.

'Your Excellency…' Alessio's private secretary hesitated for a moment. 'Are you all right?'

'Of course.' The lie slipped easily from his lips, when in truth he didn't know what 'all right' felt like. Not now. Not since he'd ejected the only person who had made him feel human again from his home.

Not ejected. She'd left. Without turning back. Without a fight. Just as she should have. He'd as good as forced her. Because he really wasn't worth fighting for.

'If you'd like a moment—?'

'No.'

Stefano grabbed the case from the floor and stood. He might be broken but he wouldn't be cowed. Some pride remained. It was hanging by the thinnest of gossamer threads, but it was there, and he clung to it because it was all he had left.

He walked into the room and Alessio's secretary slid out behind him. Shut the door with a solid click.

Alessio sat behind his desk, looking as regal as his title dictated. He'd always worn the weight of his role with distinction, born to it and accepting of it. His only flight of fancy had been his wife, Hannah. A saving grace, it seemed, because Alessio looked well.

Stefano supposed love did that to you. He wouldn't know. For him, love was simply another arrow of pain to shoot into his heart. It was as if the universe enjoyed using him for target practice.

He bowed, short and sharp. 'Your Highness.'

The words were hard to say when they had to be meant formally, rather than as a mere greeting between friends. He clenched his jaw almost hard enough to crack teeth. It all angered him. The familiar surroundings where he was now a stranger. The situation he'd created when he should have fought Alessio for what he believed was right, rather than taking matters into his own hands. Alessio too, for his silence.

There was no sign of emotion on his impassive face. He'd always been a master of control. Yet Stefano wanted him to shout and rage, as if this meant something. He wanted Alessio to care as much as he did about what had been lost.

'Your Excellency. Thank you for *finally* responding to my requests.'

Alessio didn't invite him to sit, so Stefano remained standing. Once he would have sat regardless. 'As I told your private secretary, I've recently been snowed in.'

A flicker of something passed across Alessio's face, so fleeting Stefano couldn't be sure what he'd seen.

'I hope you found a way to stay warm.'

Stefano's thoughts ran out of control with the memory of Lucy. How they'd fitted together in a way that had felt like for ever.

His breath hitched. He couldn't think of her. *Wouldn't*. Yet again she was distracting him from what he had to do.

He took a deep breath, and returned to the task he'd set himself in the months since he'd walked away from the palace. 'I assume you didn't summon me to discuss the weather?'

'It seemed the polite way to begin, since you didn't respond to any of my earlier attempts.'

Alessio's gaze slid over the violin case Stefano held in his hands. His palm was itching to release it.

'Please take a seat.'

'I'd rather stand.' Stefano placed the violin case in the middle of Alessio's desk to rid himself of the instrument, which had taken on the feeling of a time bomb on its final countdown.

'What's this?' asked Alessio.

'This is what's become of the Heart of Lasserno. A violin. A Stradivarius. Swapped for the ring in the war.'

He'd thought saying the words would change everything, but there was no lightning bolt of forgiveness from the heavens. All Stefano wanted to do was to snatch the violin and take it away from here, return it to the woman who made it sing.

Instead, he clasped his hands tight behind his back.

Alessio's eyes flared wide, then his face settled into its cool, regal demeanour once more. 'Where did you get it?'

'From a violinist. Signorina Lucy Jamieson. Her grandfather brought it home after the war. It's been with her family—'

Alessio's eyebrows rose so high they almost disappeared into his hairline. 'You *took* her violin?'

Wait... What? Alessio knew of Lucy's presence in his castle?

The surprise of that almost took his legs from underneath him. Stefano sank into the chair he'd earlier refused. 'How did you—?'

'I need to know everything that's happening in this country, so I'll never be surprised again.' The corner of Alessio's mouth curved in the merest of movements, but for him it was the equivalent of a sly smile. 'Bruno proved very informative about "the angel in the castle who is too beautiful for a devil like Moretti." They were his exact words, only partially said in jest.'

Lucy *had* been an angel. One of redemption. In the dark and lonely nights since her departure he'd had long hours to think about her time in the castle. She'd been a woman alone, trapped with a stranger. He remembered her apprehension when she'd first arrived. Of *course* she wouldn't have told him about the violin immediately. She couldn't have known how he'd react in those early days, and his terrible behaviour in the end proved any lingering fears were well justified. It had been unfair to blame her when he hadn't pursued the issue either.

In that way he wasn't a devil, as Bruno had accused. He was a vampire who'd slowly tried to suck the life and the joy from her to make himself feel better. So he could forget about his own failings and relish her attention. Which was why he'd said nothing about the coronation ring.

Still, something didn't make sense here. It was as

though he'd entered a room halfway through a conversation and had to catch up on its meaning.

'You've been…keeping an eye on me?'

'Someone had to. You weren't responding to my correspondence, and you looked like hell. Although at the time of Bruno's report I did wonder whether you were auditioning a violinist for Lasserno's orchestra in your role as patron. She would be a coup.'

His heart rate spiked at the mention of his patronage. With it, he would be able to ensure the violin's protection. Allocate funds specifically, so it remained treasured for another three hundred years.

'I'm not giving up that role too,' he said.

If he had to, his punishment would be complete.

'I'd never ask you to.' Alessio frowned, waved his hand as if in dismissal. 'But that's not important. Where is the evidence that this violin is what's become of the coronation ring?'

Alessio steepled his fingers and pinned Stefano with his steady, impassive gaze. Stefano had witnessed people wither under that assessment, which Alessio could hold unchanged until the other person cracked and divulged all their sins.

Stefano tugged at his tie…straightened it. He wasn't like those people because Alessio knew his sins. Most of them, anyhow.

'There's a story. Some diary entries.'

Lucy had left them behind on his bed when she'd gone. Stefano had yet to get to the bottom of what they meant. He still had more documents to search through from his own family's archive, although he had enough proof regarding the violin for today's meeting.

'Is there any provenance? Or only family stories about Signorina Jamieson's violin.'

'It's Lasserno's violin, not hers.' Except the words didn't ring true. They sounded hollow and false in his mouth. 'I've asked an expert to appraise it, and he believes it's a Stradivarius. Dendrochronological dating will confirm it.'

Alessio stood and moved out from behind his desk. He leaned against the front of it, his hands gripping the antique wood. The move forced Stefano to look up at him, when before they'd always treated each other as equals. In the strangest of ways, it was only now that he felt judged and found lacking. Even when he'd resigned from his position Alessio hadn't looked down on him like this.

'I knew you were strategic. Ruthless, too, if the stream of anonymous packages full of gemstones coming across my desk is anything to judge by—for which I will endlessly thank you. But I didn't realise you could be cruel.'

'She gave it to me.'

He knew he sounded like one of those whiny aristocrats who'd taken the gemstones Alessio's father had given them. They'd had no right to them, but this was different. He was doing his duty by his country, as anyone else would.

Wasn't he?

Nothing seemed certain any more. It was as if everything he'd thought he knew had shifted underneath him.

'She *gave* you a multi-million-dollar instrument that has been in her family since the war? The tool of her trade? Ask yourself why she did that, Stefano, when she could have said nothing.'

'I thought I'd fallen...'

No. It had been the right thing to do. Lucy had known in the end that the violin wasn't hers to keep and she'd left it behind. Even though he would never have stopped her if she'd picked up the case and walked away.

'I hope it sets you free...'

The pain of her last words scoured like acid through his veins. He couldn't respond to Alessio. He was struck mute by the realisation trying to break through, tapping at the inside of his consciousness like a rock hammer. He ignored it.

'I see you refuse to answer that question. So how about this one?' Alessio crossed his arms. 'What am I to do with it?'

'You said that if I found the coronation ring I could have anything I wanted.'

That was what he'd come here for. His brother and sister. He'd forgotten them somewhere in the conversation, since it wasn't going the way he'd expected.

'That was youthful rambling, when we were both insecure about our place in the world we'd been thrown into too early and underprepared. I never required *this*.' He motioned to the violin case on the desk. 'All you've ever needed to do is ask me for what you want. So what is it?'

Stefano wanted so many things. He wanted his brother and sister to be free of the weight of his family's obligation to the Crown. He wanted his friendship with Alessio to be repaired. He wanted...what he couldn't have. What he'd pushed away.

Better to ask for something which could be granted than wish for something that couldn't. 'I want you to free Gino and Emilia.'

Alessio's eyes widened. 'Your brother and sister aren't my prisoners.'

'Both want to travel overseas for work. That means leaving their roles here.'

'They go with my blessing.' Alessio rolled his eyes in a way that was entirely uncharacteristic and no part of his normally regal demeanour. 'Is this really how bad things have become between us? I thought I'd created a modern principality, whereas your family believes we're trapped in some medieval realm. It seems I'm failing as a benevolent monarch—but at least I have a priceless violin. Thank you for small blessings.'

Stefano's anger spiked then, mingled with the pain of the things he'd thrown away. A picture of his last moments with Lucy was filling his head. Her face... How wounded she'd been...

He launched himself from his seat, unable to sit still, to sit being...*judged*. Alessio leaned back a little to let him pass, as if Stefano might lash out. It made him wonder how he looked, because in this moment he felt feral. He began to pace, to burn off the excess energy that welled inside, clawing at him, wanting to tear free.

'Doesn't *any* of this matter to you?'

'Many things matter. Love, friendship. The rest is ephemeral. Right now, you're trying to buy redemption. Trust me—redemption won't come until you've forgiven yourself.'

Stefano stared at the man who had once been his

closest friend. Everything ached, as if nothing would sit right with him ever again.

Alessio sighed. 'Hannah warned me about writing missives, but I didn't know how else to reach you when you wouldn't take my calls. I've failed as a monarch and now as a friend. I should have listened to your counsel. You were right about the press. So what do you need to end this distance between us? Because I miss you. Hannah misses you.'

Stefano stopped dead, not sure of what he was hearing. 'It can't be this easy.'

'None of it has been. I've been enraged, hurt—and confused by what you did. You blindsided me. But in the end I've learned a great deal about love, generosity and forgiveness from my wife. Though I *would* appreciate another grovelling apology.' Alessio smirked. 'It only seems right.'

Of all the things to be asked of him, an apology was the easiest to give. Stefano walked over to Alessio and stood in front of him, head bowed, paying due respect to his monarch and to the friend he'd wronged. 'I'm sorry. I've regretted my actions every day since I walked from this room.'

'I guessed. Locking yourself in your castle and taking to Lasserno's aristocracy like an avenging angel suggested a great deal of contrition. But that's in the past. It's time to turn to the present and the future. Now you've told me what your siblings want, what do *you* want? Your old job?'

Stefano rocked back on his heels. Months ago this would have been like an answer to his every prayer.

Now…? Now nothing seemed right without Lucy in his life.

'No.'

Alessio flinched, pain etched over his face. Stefano didn't wish to hurt his friend again, but he needed to find his future rather than step back into the past, which was what Alessio offered.

'The things I want aren't in your power to grant, because they involve someone else.'

Lucy. She was all he desired. Since she'd left the castle he'd been plunged into a silence so stark that in the absence of her music it was as if he was the only living being left on earth.

'Ah… I think I know where you are and I sympathise,' Alessio said. 'Though I do have a request. Hannah's due to give birth any day, and we want you as the godfather of our child. I have a suspicion she's holding on until you say yes…until I make this right.'

The roiling emotions inside Stefano stilled. He was having trouble making sense of the question—such a privilege being asked of him after all that had passed between them.

Then those words of Celine's crept back, whispering in his ear… 'What if I'm not worthy of the role?'

'Listen to what I'm saying.' Alessio laid his hand on Stefano's shoulder, the comfort of one friend to another. 'You're worth more than you ever knew. I'm sorry that you ever felt less, but you are and will remain my closest friend. I don't care about your role as Shield of the Crown, or your title. It was your friendship that I needed, and you gave me that unfailingly. What you did—misplaced as it was—freed me to follow my heart with Hannah. Although the execution was poor, your intentions were good, and in the end that's all that matters.'

   'Intention is everything.'

They were Lucy's words. She'd been right. He should have listened to her. Instead he'd cast her aside, because he hadn't been able to trust or forgive himself. He'd been inexcusably cruel when she'd handed him his means of salvation. She'd handed *everything* to him, without asking for anything in return, and he'd thrown it back in her face.

Stefano couldn't ignore the truth. He loved her. He didn't deserve her.

And yet if Alessio could forgive him, then perhaps Lucy could too.

CHAPTER ELEVEN

BRIGHT LIGHTS BORE down on her as Lucy stood on the stage. The applause from the Parisian crowd was thunderous as she took a deep bow. She'd been asked to perform a single concert on a Stradivarius that was being sold by a consortium, to showcase the instrument for potential purchasers. By the measure of the applause she'd done the violin justice.

It had been an extraordinary instrument to play— a thrill all its own—but it hadn't been *hers*. The tone was still magical, but subtly different, without the same sense of wonder and joy attached to every note.

It had been easy enough, though, to pour the emotions of grief and loss into the mournful music she'd played. Once, she'd thought she understood those feelings. Yet until she'd walked away from Stefano she'd had *no* real idea of pain's true depths. They'd had so little time together, and still his impact was like being hit by a meteor.

World-ending.

She was left with a deep and unrelenting ache. Missing him. Missing her violin.

She had many regrets, but in the end leaving the violin she'd played for years was not one of them. Her father was furious, but he and his solicitors couldn't argue against the evidence. The violin was Lasserno's heart, and she'd given it back. It was now safe from a fate similar to that of the violin she'd just performed with: being seen as an investment rather than the treasure it was.

She wondered if another violinist played it now, in Lasserno's orchestra, or whether it was locked in a glass case somewhere, on display for all the world to see, with the story of the coronation ring and her grandfather.

The loss of Stefano and the violin was woven into the fabric of her recent past. She didn't understand how she could unravel it, so all she did was stand there, basking in the acclamation of the crowd, until the applause died away.

Her time was done. She took her final bow and went backstage, handing the Stradivarius to a team of security guards, who locked it back in its case and whisked it away. She accepted congratulations, said goodbye to those in the ensemble who'd played with her, and then exited through the stage door.

A small crowd stood there waiting for her. She smiled. Signed autographs on programmes until the well-wishers thinned. If she'd been carrying her own violin she would have found some transport to take her back to her accommodation. But tonight she would walk.

It was a cool evening, with a chill reminiscent of the mountain castle which had changed her for ever. She wanted that chill to seep into her bones. A reminder of what she'd lost in those beautiful, frozen days in Lasserno.

As she stepped away from the stage door, ready to walk to the boutique hotel the organisers had arranged for her, she glimpsed a final person standing in the shadows, waiting. She readied herself with one more smile for one more autograph. Then the person stepped out of the darkness into the light.

Stefano.

He stood immaculate in a dinner suit, white shirt and black bow tie. The cloth lovingly clasped every inch of his impressive frame. The perfection of his suit was in vivid contrast to the rest of him. His hair was more unruly than she'd seen it before, teasing the neck of his collar. And the ever-present shadow of stubble on his face was now more of a beard. The temptation to reach out, to touch and see if it still prickled under her fingers, almost overwhelmed her. Instead, she clenched her fists tight.

'Your performance was magnificent,' he said in a voice that was rough, as if he'd almost forgotten how to speak—just like that first day she'd met him in the doorway of his castle, looking like some gothic hero.

But he wasn't any kind of hero. He was just a man. And she knew that her performance, the emotion and the ache of it, had all been down to losing him.

'Thank you.'

She wondered if he'd heard it in her music. What he'd thought if he had.

A sharp breeze gusted down the narrow street past the stage door. She trembled, but not from the cold. Stefano blazed in front of her. He'd always been heat enough to keep her warm. She dug her fingers reflexively into the palm of her hand.

A deep frown interrupted his brow as Stefano took a step forward. 'Are you hurting?'

Hurting? The ache was relentless—almost like a living thing, gnawing at her insides, day after day. If not for her music it would have broken her irretrievably. And, yes, she still felt as if parts of her were missing.

Lucy took half a step back. Better that than running into his strong arms and hoping he'd catch her when she fell against him.

'I'm doing fine.'

That was the partial truth. She wasn't hurting herself in a quest for perfection, or at the demand of another, because she realised now that she was *enough*. She always had been. And she deserved someone who could love her with an open heart. No artifice. No agenda.

She was someone with a warm heart herself, brimming to give away some of the love it held. This man in front of her didn't believe that he could give her that… that he was deserving of what she offered. And she wanted the love, the adoration… Everything she believed she'd experienced in a week trapped in a castle with him.

'What are you doing here, Stefano?'

'I came here for your performance. I came here to see you.'

Her heart jumped as if it had been shocked. Behind her, light spilled onto the road as the stage door opened. A few of her fellow musicians came out, stopped.

'You okay, Lucy? Sure you won't come for a drink?'

This was her perfect escape. She could leave with these people whose company she'd come to enjoy and escape Stefano for ever.

But she needed closure. She hadn't had it when she'd fled Castello Varno in those icy mountains. When a sympathetic Bruno had heeded her call, picking her up and driving her to the *pensione*. Maybe seeing Stefano would help plaster over her damaged heart—because whilst she hadn't been broken, she'd been left emotionally bruised and bloody.

'No, thanks. I'm fine,' she replied. 'I've got things to do.'

They nodded. Said their final goodbyes. Stared at Stefano.

He didn't acknowledge them at all. His gaze didn't leave her. It was intense, almost...*hungry*. Scanning over her as if he was looking for missing pieces. He shouldn't look for them here. She'd left them behind in his castle, when she'd walked out through the great wooden doors trying not to look back to see if Stefano was watching her.

'Allow me to give you a lift to your hotel.'

He motioned to a black limousine, which sat cloaked in darkness. She shook her head. Standing metres away from him was bad enough. She'd never cope being cooped up in the cabin of a car with him.

'It's a nice night and it's not far.'

Lucy looked up at the sky. The lights of the city obliterated most of the stars. Unlike in Varno, at Stefano's castle, where on that clear night on the ramparts she'd felt as if she could reach out and touch heaven. And then afterwards, in the turret with him, she had.

'I'll walk.'

She needed to work off the performance. The adrenaline of the concert still coursed through her blood, leav-

ing her light-headed. Reckless. That wasn't a safe way
to be around Stefano.

'Would you allow me to walk with you?'

Whilst she always felt safe in Paris, it still seemed
like the sensible thing to do, and she needed to find out
why he was here. Curiosity won. She hoped it didn't
kill this cat…

'Sure. Why not?' Lucy let out a slow breath and
wrapped her arms around her waist.

Stefano stepped forward. Stopped. 'Are you cold?
Would you like my jacket?'

'I'm…'

He reached for his button, undid it. Shrugged out of
the fine black wool with its satin lapels. He approached
her with some hesitation. She didn't object. Partly because she was cold and had forgotten a wrap. But partly
simply wanting him to be close, if only for a few moments.

He draped his jacket gently round her shoulders and
the warmth of the fabric from the heat of his own body
engulfed her. The scent of him was crisp as winter,
dark as spice.

When he stepped away, his eyes glittered like black
diamonds in the streetlights. 'I know you don't like to
be cold.'

'Thank you.' The sting behind her eyelids hinted
at threatening tears, but crying would get her nothing
other than puffy eyes and a red nose. 'Let's go.'

She began to walk, thankful for the ballet flats she
wore. He turned and caught up with her in a few easy
strides.

'You're looking…well,' he said.

A tiny spark of pleasure lit inside her, but she knew he was only being kind. She looked haggard. The dark rings under her eyes from sleepless nights were not so well hidden by make-up. In the nights since leaving Lasserno she'd done a great deal of thinking—about him, her life, her career... None of it had been easy.

'As are you.'

There was more truth in her comment than in his, even though something about him appeared wild. His frame was leaner than it had been all those weeks before.

He made a noise like a snort. A scornful sound, as if he hated this stilted formality between them as much as she did.

The people of Paris bustled about them. The city of love was still alive at this time of night. It left a bitter tang in her mouth, a clench of pain deep inside her, that here she was with the man she'd fallen in love with and there was nothing here for her.

But it wasn't all wasted.

She'd recognised a thing or two after she'd left the violin with Stefano. When she'd played in her orchestra on her return...played here tonight. It wasn't the instrument that defined her. She was good at what she did on her own, no matter how much she missed playing the violin that had become like a part of her.

'You're back with your orchestra.'

Stefano didn't ask it as a question, and a tiny thrill ran through her at his knowledge of what she'd been doing before she shut it down. Her return had been on the orchestra's web page for anyone to see. Still, he'd checked...

'I am.'

'Did you have any trouble?'

'I took back what was rightfully mine.'

She'd refused to accept the way she'd been treated. Made it clear the injury was no fault of her own and any rumours were just that. Without proof. She liked to think that in the end everyone had seen through the lies. What she hadn't expected was the support from some of the other members of the orchestra who valued her leadership. Then there had been the letters from fans, wishing her well in her recovery, waiting impatiently for her return.

'And how is it?' he asked.

They'd almost reached her hotel. She would say goodnight to him and then they'd part. He was on his own journey, she was on hers, and they didn't converge. All she had left was the empty space in her heart where he had been, which tonight she'd filled with music. She'd return to Salzburg and they'd both move on.

She didn't know why that thought felt like a death.

'I'm thinking of resigning my position,' she said.

'No! Lucy, you can't. Has that *bastardo* Viktor—?'

'It has nothing to do with him.'

Stefano's vehement defence sent another shiver of awareness through her, but she couldn't allow it to mean anything. He'd made himself clear the day she'd walked out of his life and back to her own.

'I wouldn't resign for that man—not after I've fought to keep my position. The fact I'm back at the orchestra shows his undermining of me didn't work. In the end I won. He lost.'

She realised the truth of that now. But, more importantly, she knew she needed to work with people who wanted to create something beautiful rather than people who'd stab each other in the back trying to improve their position. In that way, deciding on her future was becoming easier.

'Of course he did. I've looked at some of his playing. He can't match you—in *any* way.'

The passion contained in those words slid through her veins, sparking flares of heat deep inside. But there was nothing for it. They'd arrived at her hotel. Now she and Stefano would part, and that would be the end of them. She would be gracious, even though her insides felt as if they were being shredded by razor blades.

'That's kind, but we're at my hotel.' She looked at the doorman and smiled at him as he held the door open for her.

'Mademoiselle Jamieson. Your Excellency.'

She turned to Stefano. 'How does he know you?'

Stefano slipped his hands into the pockets of his trousers, shrugged. 'I'm staying here as well.'

Lucy hesitated. The tumble of emotions inside her was strange and confusing. 'That's kind of creepy, Stefano.'

'You've made that accusation before. It appears I do "creepy" quite well—even though it wasn't my intention, and there are good reasons for my being here.'

'Staying at the same hotel as me should have been where you started our conversation. Could you not have said something earlier, like back at the concert hall?'

'You would have found out soon enough. And I was enjoying the walk with you.'

She strode through the foyer and to the lift. Slipped

off his jacket and handed it to him. He looked at it for a moment and frowned, as if the thought of her returning it almost hurt. Still, after some hesitation he took it, and folded it over his arm.

'It's been nice seeing you, Stefano, but I've had a long day. I wish you all the best for your future. Goodnight.'

He flinched, and she didn't care. She couldn't allow herself any kind of softer feeling, like sympathy, since he had none for her.

'I... I want to keep talking. Could we take this to my room?'

Her heart did a silly backflip, but she ignored it. Frowned. 'What for?'

How could she go to his room when all she wanted to do was fall into his arms and be held?

'Because there's a lot that I have to say, and it's clear my attempts so far have been poor.'

'I don't owe you any more of my time.'

Seeing him again had brought all that pain she'd tried locking down into sharp relief. She'd set a clock on her grief over Stefano. Six months. Six months in which she'd immersed herself in it and hoped not to drown. Now she'd seen him again that clock had restarted, and the day she'd walked out through the door of his castle came back with the fresh, bright sting of a papercut.

She stabbed at the button for the lift, needing to get away.

'No, you don't owe me anything,' Stefano said, keeping his voice low as a few people in the foyer were watching them both. 'However, I owe you a *great* deal. Please, Lucy.'

* * *

At a distance in the concert hall, she'd looked luminous. Playing the instrument like an angel. Stefano had almost wanted to purchase the violin, to capture its heavenly beauty, but it was only wood and strings. The real genius was Lucy.

He wished he could trap it, bottle it.

Keep it to himself.

Never let it go.

But there was a saying about loving someone and setting them free. In that her grandfather had been wrong.

Stefano knew he hadn't been able to hold her and keep her before because he'd been in no fit state to offer her anything. He only hoped he was better now, because her absence in his life had left a hole so great nothing could fill it. He'd thought the chasm between himself and Alessio bad enough. It was a mere crack in the pavement compared to this. Without Lucy, his life seemed wholly lacking, and he had no idea if he could fix what he'd deliberately, callously broken.

'We don't owe each other anything, Stefano. If you feel an obligation to me in any way, I'm releasing you from it.'

'I only want to talk.'

And he hoped that words would be enough. Though he'd already hurt her terribly with his words. Words not meant. Words spat out in fear because of self-loathing. He knew his actions would need to match the true meaning of what he said tonight *exactly*, or he would lose her for ever.

If he hadn't lost her already.

'If I come up to your room and listen to what you have to say, will you then leave me alone?'

'Of course.'

Every part of him objected to his promise, but if all he could ever have of her was her music, then that would be enough. It had to be. He'd become her most ardent yet silent supporter.

'There are conditions.'

She stood there so fierce, dressed all in black—presumably so nothing would detract from the music she played—but all he could see was *her*. She filled the foyer of the hotel, luminous with her strawberry blonde hair in a flawless chignon, her honey eyes glowing with a furious fire. How everyone in this space was not as transfixed as he was, he could not explain.

'Whatever you want, Lucy.'

She looked stricken. 'You stay on your side of the room. I stay on mine.'

For a moment, hope flared. If she didn't want to be close to him then maybe she felt it too—the indefinable, shimmering desire between them. And, whilst she looked magnificent, no amount of make-up could hide the bruised shadows under her eyes, which Stefano was sure *he'd* caused.

He craved to touch her, comfort her, soothe away her pain. But he'd hold those demands of hers sacrosanct. It was a small price to pay if it allowed him to say what he needed to. And when he had, he'd open his arms and hope she'd walk into them.

Not sure of his voice in this moment, he nodded.

'I need the words, Stefano.'

'I accept your conditions.'

The antique lift door rattled open. Her eyes widened, almost as if in fear, and then she went ahead of him. He keyed in the number for his floor as she took one corner, fixing her gaze resolutely on the moving numbers as the door clanked shut before them. He stood in the other corner, closing his eyes so he didn't have to watch those same numbers pass him by like a terrible countdown.

Probably to the end…hopefully to the beginning.

The lift eased to a stop and he followed Lucy out to the only door—that of the Presidential Suite. He opened it and motioned for her to go inside. She entered, then stopped. A mountain of a man rose from a chair. He'd forgotten about the security guard following him, and saw Lucy stare at him with concern.

'You may go now,' Stefano said. 'I'll call with further instructions if required.'

The man nodded. 'Of course, Your Excellency.'

'Please excuse the necessary security,' Stefano said, as Lucy watched the man leave. He took himself to the furthest corner of the room, since that was what she wanted, and draped his jacket over the couch. 'Would you like something to drink? I can call for tea, coffee… hot chocolate?'

'This isn't a social visit. You said you had things to say.'

She crossed her arms, standing straight and tall just inside the closed door of the room, but her voice… He could hear the desperation of it. Then her watchful gaze looked him up and down. Did she want him still? It was time he played the cards he'd been dealt. He hoped it was a good enough hand.

'I have a message from His Royal Highness.'

'Are you speaking again?'

'Yes.'

If there had been one moment of relief in the disaster of these past months, it was that. His friendship with Alessio had been healed over a long night of dinner and of talking in a way they hadn't for years. If it was possible, their friendship had deepened. He was even going to be godfather to the beautiful little princess born two days after he'd accepted the honour.

Once he would have thought his life was perfect, but now he knew it wasn't. Not yet.

'Has he given you your job back?' she asked.

'His Highness has a perfectly good private secretary. It's not a role I want. Not any more.'

Right now, he couldn't think of any future without Lucy in it. He'd told Alessio as much, and his friend had understood. Stefano couldn't contemplate a life without her. They'd only been together for the briefest of times, and yet already it seemed that they were inevitable. His whole future lay in her brilliant hands.

He had done so much to hurt her, and if he could re-visit those last days, he would change everything. He saw now that they'd both been afraid because they'd found something precious and yet both of them had held knowledge that could tear them apart. By taking the Stradivarius he'd thought he'd found the means to his salvation. Whereas if he'd really understood the truth he would have seen that salvation only came from within himself.

'What *do* you want, Stefano?'

Her.

Always. Only. Ever.

'His Highness asked me the same question…' All he could offer Lucy was a polite smile. Telling the truth now might have her running away from him. 'But I have an offer from him for you. Please wait here.'

He walked into his bedroom, grabbed the case that had been sitting carefully on his bed. Hoped that this would at least put the spark back in her eyes—the one he'd seen that first moment when he'd opened the door to his castle and found her on the doorstep. The bright gleam he'd witnessed when he'd moved inside her as they'd made love…when he'd shown her the stars.

On his return to the sitting room, Lucy stood looking out of the windows, staring over the city of love. The place where he hoped he could show her what she meant to him.

She turned, and her eyes widened when she saw what he held. Her fingers flexed.

'I've been asked by His Royal Highness Prince Alessio of Lasserno to bring this to you. On permanent loan from our country.'

He placed the case on a coffee table, opened it with the reverence such a precious instrument deserved. The Stradivarius lay in all its burnished glory inside. In the end a committee of experts had examined it with excitement and confirmed what they had all known. They had assured everyone that it was still perfect, before returning it to its rightful owner.

Because he'd come to an understanding, after reading her grandfather's diary entries and researching more of his family's papers—out of love, not anger or desperation—that this violin was as much a part of a love story as an object of salvation from the war. A decent man would have let her keep it when she'd offered it to him, but somewhere in those bleak months he'd lost his humanity…lost himself.

It had taken Lucy to help him find himself again.

'Is this…?'

Her voice was breathless, choked. Tears sparkled in her eyes. It took all his willpower not to go to her, but he'd made a promise and he wouldn't break it. He'd broken too much already.

'Your violin.'

'It's not mine.'

'It is if you want it. My country will provide permanent security, so it never feels like a burden. It will always be safe and so will you.'

Her eyes were wide, staring at the open case. A tear dripped onto her cheek and she scrubbed it away. 'Why?'

He stood firm in his place even as her tears continued to fall unchecked. Not until she asked would he approach her, and if she never did then here was where he'd stay till she walked out through the door.

'You solved a mystery. You brought a part of my country's history back to us—even if it wasn't the coronation ring I'd been searching for. You brought a story of my family and yours. A story of love and wartime. The diary extracts you left for me tell part of the tale, but there's more.'

He hoped it would give her an explanation, and put her grandfather's memory to rest with some peace.

'Your grandfather's diary said, *"The violin is Lasserno's heart, not mine. Mine belongs to another."* I believe the precious object being taken to safety by your grandfather as the enemy marched towards the castle was not a ring. It was a person. My great-aunt.'

Lucy gripped the back of an elegant brocade armchair in one hand, wiping away tears with the other. The shock and the pain of seeing Stefano again and now this? She didn't know what to do. She wanted to walk to her violin, take it and run. But she also wanted to run to Stefano and fling herself into his arms.

All those conflicting emotions had her frozen, hanging onto the chair, because she wasn't sure that her legs would carry her if she tried to move.

'How did you work that out?'

'You told me your grandfather had talked of another woman. One of his diary entries said, *"We used Lasserno's heart to save ourselves, yet I couldn't save Betty."* That was a clue. With the Australians' love of shortening names I wondered if Betty might be a reference to my great-aunt Elisabetta. In my search for answers about the ring I'd scoured my great-grandfather's papers. It wasn't until I saw your grandfather's diary entries that I thought of looking for any of hers.'

'What did you find?'

'Not as much as I'd hoped. A few notes on scraps of paper, tucked into the cover of a book recording the birthdays of my family members over the generations. Some words of love and admiration in handwriting that looked like your grandfather's. Was Arthur's birthday the sixteenth of March?'

Tears filled her eyes again, spilled onto her cheeks. She wiped them away, nodding, unable to speak.

'His name is in that book. I'm sure she never meant to forget him.'

'You said she died in the war?' Her voice trembled and broke.

Stefano nodded. 'I told you she wasn't spoken of much. Grief gives some people the need to recollect, and others the wish to forget. My family were in the latter category. From what I could piece together, it seems Elisabetta was a bright, bold young woman, who did not like Lasserno's neutrality in the war when she'd witnessed so much suffering elsewhere. But even more information came from your grandfather. Having his true name meant my investigations could determine his service number, and with that I was able to search your country's archives. Your grandfather wrote a report to his superiors, explaining his time on the run.'

Lucy's breath hitched. She and her mother had never thought to look into her grandfather's war records. The shock of the diaries had been enough. Nothing else had entered their minds.

'What did it say?'

'His report told the story of his time in Lasserno, being sheltered by my family. He fled with my great-aunt, who'd helped people via the underground movement before, making her a target. They were caught in a firefight and Elisabetta was injured by shrapnel. He tried to save her, but she was mortally wounded. Arthur had to keep running so he wouldn't be captured. He reported that Elisabetta's remains were taken by members of the underground movement who said they would inform my great-grandfather.'

'Anything about the coronation ring?'

'Not as such.'

'I'm sorry.'

Stefano shrugged. 'It's more than I've ever had before. More than I could have imagined. You gave that to me. To my country. Arthur mentions the violin and his playing, which allowed him and Elisabetta to hide their identities. He doesn't say how he acquired it—however, your guess that he swapped one precious object for another fits. How else would he have obtained a Stradivarius? It's what I would have done to save the one I loved.'

His gaze was fixed on her with an intensity which made Lucy light-headed.

'In my family's documents I also found this.' Stefano reached into his pocket and pulled out a yellowed piece of paper. He handed it to her. 'A letter.'

She took the thin, worn document and opened it to read the neat black script that looked a lot like the writing in her grandfather's diaries. It was dated after the war ended, and addressed to the then Count of Varno.

I am sorry for everything precious of yours that I could not save. Forgive me. For I will never forgive myself.

There was no signature, just the initial 'A', but it was enough. She looked at Stefano, who had a soft and tender smile on his face.

'My grandfather carried guilt over this his whole life, and never more than in his final days,' she said. 'It was awful. He kept saying, "I'm sorry." We didn't know what for.'

'I never understood why your grandfather, a stranger, would have been entrusted with something so precious as the country's coronation ring. But the story comes together if Elisabetta died trying to get the ring to safety, whilst your grandfather was trying to protect them both. I'm sure he loved her, and she loved him.'

'All those times he talked to me of holding on to love and never letting it go… I wonder if he couldn't face your family because of the shame of losing your great-aunt. That's what he was asking forgiveness for—especially if they were in love.'

In a terrible, heart-breaking way it all made sense.

'It wouldn't surprise me,' Stefano said. 'Even if it wasn't your fault, losing someone you loved and were meant to protect would plague you with guilt for eternity.'

In the soft light of the room Stefano's dark eyes glowed with a banked heat which lit inside her too. No matter how cold it was, he'd always kept her warm. Then he held out his arms, almost like an offering for her to come to him.

'So here we are. Two people brought together by this story.'

As much as his open arms were a temptation, Lucy held her ground. The reason he'd come to Paris was to deliver the violin. Without it she would never have seen him again, she was sure. He didn't really want her. He certainly hadn't trusted her. She wondered if he would trust anyone. Something about that crushed her heart like the wings of a doomed butterfly.

'The story you've given me is a beautiful one.

Thank you. And now your job's done you can go back to Lasserno.'

She wouldn't subject herself to more pain, to more hope for the heart of a man who probably still hadn't found his own. Who didn't know what he wanted out of life. Because she'd asked and he'd had no answer. He certainly didn't want *her*.

'My job here has only just started, *tesoro*.'

Her eyes widened at the endearment which had slipped out unchecked, and his gentle words slid under her ribs like a knife, stabbing at her with a hope she shouldn't have.

'Don't think too hard, Stefano. Let's just agree that I was rebound girl, and you were rebound guy. A palate cleanser—even though I did get left with a nasty taste in my mouth at the end.'

He shook his head. 'If you're deliberately trying to hurt me, you're succeeding. But take comfort that nothing you say can hurt me more than I have hurt myself. I was a fool to realise too late that you'd stolen a piece of my heart. And now I'm offering all of it. Because whilst I don't deserve you, I cannot help having fallen in love with you.'

Her breath caught. There might not be enough oxygen in the room to fill her lungs after such a declaration.

'But wasn't what happened between us all a lie?'

She'd tried not to believe his cruel words *'What we did had nothing to do with love.'* On those dark nights alone she'd thought of their time together. The things he'd done for her. His kindness. She desperately wanted to believe that it had come from somewhere deeper, a true caring, but it hurt too much to allow that fantasy in the unforgiving light of day.

'I told myself lies about many things. About how without my role as Alessio's private secretary I was nothing. How I could never be forgiven for what I'd done. How there was no one I could trust. But the worst lies I told myself were about us. I ignored that what I felt for you was the one truth—the one thing I should have trusted. Instead, fear won. My decisions had been so poor. Talking to the press about Alessio... Even my engagement... Because it's clear Celine never genuinely loved me. How could I trust my feelings for you when I couldn't trust myself?'

She wrapped her arms around her waist. A trembling had started through her body and it wouldn't stop. Not cold. Not fear. Just a well of emotion she didn't know what to do with. So she tried to hold it in. If she let it out—if she *hoped*—she didn't know how to survive rejection again.

'But how can *I* trust what you're saying is true?'

'There is one reason I haven't accepted any role from Alessio. I can't contemplate a life without you in it. I don't know what shape it can take. This is not meant as pressure, but to explain. You're not responsible for me, Lucy. You're not responsible for my happiness. But I can only decide what I'm going to do when I know what you want too—because I love you with all that I have.'

This was everything she'd craved, and yet she was terrified to reach out and take what she thought he might be offering. 'I don't know if I trust *myself*. My choices haven't been great either.'

'You were betrayed. It leaves scars. But a wise friend said to me, *"Many things matter. Love, friendship. The rest is ephemeral."* Trust in the way I feel for you. Trust in my love for you. That's what I know. That's what I'm sure of. But I'll wait until you feel those things yourself. I'll follow wherever you wish to lead me to make that happen. I want you to be my future…if that's what you want too.'

He stood under the lights as if spot-lit on a stage. Delivering a soliloquy that spoke to her alone, filling her with light and warmth and something that felt a lot like the hope she'd thought she might never find again.

'What are you asking?'

'I'm asking you to be with me.'

He dropped to his knees as if in slow motion. This magnificent, proud man was on the floor over at the other side of the room. His focus only on her.

'To marry me, if you'll have me. To be the Countess of my heart and my home. All I have to give you is the man. I hope he can be enough. Because I am only half a man without you, Lucy. You are my missing pieces.'

She couldn't stand still. She rounded the armchair, walked towards Stefano, trying not to run. When she reached him he looked up at her, and she saw the love she felt for him mirrored in the dark heat of his gaze. She cupped his cheeks in her hands. The weeks-long stubble there teased her fingertips.

'You were enough before, and you're even more so now with that declaration.'

He shut his eyes for a moment, then opened them again. They glinted in the lights of the room, brimming and full. One overflowed, a tear tracking from its corner.

She wiped it away with her thumb. 'You said you don't cry.'

'Only for you. You break me, Lucy. The day you left, the music in my heart died.'

He could break her too. Her own vision began to blur, but these weren't tears of sadness. 'Oh, Stefano.'

'May I touch you now?'

His voice was raw with emotion, quiet and cracked. As cracked as she felt. But she hoped that in each other's arms they could put themselves back together again.

'Please.'

He stood, wrapped her tight as she nestled against his hot, hard chest. It was as if everything was right once more. Whole and perfect. She breathed in the scent of him, cool and crisp with a hint of spice. He would remind her of winter for ever. It might become her favourite season…

'I have something for you.' He murmured the words into her hair. 'It's in my jacket, but I need to let you go to reach it.'

She looked up at him. Traced her fingers against his beautiful mouth. His lips parted. 'I've only just got back into your arms.'

Stefano kissed her fingertips, then loosened his embrace. 'It'll be for a moment. Then I'll be back and never let you go again.'

He went to the jacket draped over the arm of the couch and reached inside, came back to her holding an antique leather ring box. He opened it. Inside lay an extravagant ring. A large oval diamond surrounded by a halo of smaller round diamonds. It sparkled under the lights of the room, pristine and white, like fresh-fallen snow in the sunshine.

'I wanted something that shone as brightly as you. To show you how much you've brought to my life. You've brought music, you've brought happiness, but most importantly you've brought love. *Ti amo*, Lucy. Be mine.'

She smiled, her heart so full of love for this man that she wasn't sure there was room left for anything else. 'I already am. I've never stopped.'

Stefano moved back, giving himself a little space, and gently slipped the ring onto her finger. The perfect fit celebrated the bright new bond between them.

Then Lucy placed her hand over his heart, which beat strong and sure under her palm, marking out the tempo of their love. 'How could I not marry the man who showed me the stars again?'

EPILOGUE

LUCY WALKED TOWARDS the giant Christmas tree that stood in the corner of Castello Varno's sitting room. As the new Contessa, she'd spent a month decorating for the season. All Stefano's staff had joined her with enthusiasm, saying it had been too long since the castle had seen a proper Christmas.

She adjusted a few glittering silver stars, a strand of tinsel, as the gentle chords from a distant piano drifted into the room. Stefano had begun taking lessons soon after their engagement had been announced.

Her heart swelled with pride as she heard the song he was learning in order to accompany her at Lasserno's New Year's Eve Royal Gala Ball. Whilst she was guest violinist for a few pieces with the orchestra that night, their personal surprise was to be their playing of the first movement of Monti's "Czardas" together, for the crowd.

Almost nothing had been so special as those moments practising together, when she and Stefano had been able to share their love of music. The only thing eclipsing it had been their wedding, a little over twelve months earlier, in Lasserno's Cathedral.

It had been a celebration befitting the Count of Varno, Shield of the Crown. But to her it had seemed surprisingly intimate, even if they had married in front of hundreds of people. Alessio had walked her down the long aisle that day. She'd never forget the words he'd murmured to her before moving to Stefano's side as his best man, in that moment showing his enduring support for her beloved husband.

'I am so glad you found him...for us all.'

She was glad she'd found him too—in more ways than she could ever express. Stefano's presence in her life had restored her trust. With him, it never wavered. The promises he made were always kept.

He'd followed her to Salzburg, wanting her to be sure that the decision to leave her role as first violin was one she was happy with, and in no way influenced by him. In the six months they had been there he'd helped her take back the whole city for herself.

His siblings had happily put their own desires on hold to care for the castle whilst allowing him time to be himself. Not the Count of Varno. Not the Shield of the Crown and Alessio's confidant. Simply Stefano Moretti, the man she loved.

She hadn't noticed that silence had fallen, lost in her own thoughts. The door to the sitting room opened and Stefano walked inside. Goosebumps skittered over her. Each time she saw him she had the same thrill as the first, when he'd opened the castle door to her and in many ways opened the door to the rest of her life.

'I thought you'd be toasting marshmallows,' he said.

She placed her hand on her stomach and laughed. 'I think I've been eating too many.'

His eyes flared with banked heat. 'You've certainly been taking to winter activities with great enthusiasm.'

'I've realised it's a wonderful season if you spend it with the right person.'

A sultry heat of her own flushed her cheeks. She'd come to learn that there were many ways to spend a cold, snowy day. Stefano seemed determined never to let her be cold again.

The corners of his mouth rose into a wicked smile which curled her toes. 'Nice to know you believe you made the right choice.'

'You're learning a complicated piece for the piano to join me in playing before your country. Who else would do that for me?'

He chuckled, and the sound rippled right through her in glorious waves of pleasure. 'I hope I do you justice.'

His piano teacher said Stefano had real talent. But whilst *she* knew he had nothing to worry about, Lucy understood his fears, because the first time she'd performed in front of a crowd she'd been terrified.

She went to him, stood on her toes, and gently kissed his lips in encouragement. 'You're wonderful and your playing is wonderful.'

He slid his arms around her waist and deepened the kiss, holding her tight. All of the man was hard, but now he was a little bit compromising—at least where she was concerned.

Lucy fell into the kiss, into him, and relished those precious moments before pulling back.

Stefano's breathing was heavy, his breath gusting against her cheek. 'Why stop?'

She laughed. 'Later. I want to give you your Christmas present.'

'Now?'

Her heart thumped a little harder as she went to the tree and grabbed a small rectangular box from underneath, which she'd only wrapped and placed there that morning.

'Before everyone arrives.'

Stefano's family was joining them for Christmas Eve the following day, and staying until it was time to leave for the capital and the ball. She loved his brother and sister, but she wanted these next precious moments to be shared with her husband alone.

She handed him the gift and he took it from her.

Shook it. The box rattled. He raised an eyebrow. 'Do I get a hint?'

She took his hand. 'No. Come and open it.'

He twined his fingers with hers in a gentle squeeze as she led him to the couch. They sat in front of the fire and Stefano turned his attention to the wrapping.

Lucy swallowed, her mouth dry. It was silly to be nervous, but every day she tried to make Stefano happy, to remind him that he was a good man. That he was loved.

He tugged at the silver bow, picked at the tape, and carefully peeled open the green paper, leaving him with a plain white box. Lifting the lid, he stared inside. His eyes widened, and then the plastic stick it contained, with its two prominent blue lines, tumbled to the floor.

'Tesoro...' Stefano jumped from the chair and gathered her into his arms once more. 'La mia stella.'

My star.

She'd begun to have suspicions a few weeks earlier that her expanding cleavage, which Stefano loved so much, had less to do with the toasted marshmallows and hot chocolate she'd been consuming and more to do with the fact that on some days they'd been casual with contraception.

Stefano cupped her face in his hands. 'You have been looking more beautiful than ever. I thought it was happiness…' His voice was filled with wonder, a reverent whisper. 'But this is more than I could have dreamed. How far along are you?'

Tears pricked at her eyes. This was more than she could have dreamed too—the joy that filled her in this moment. 'Still early…maybe five or six weeks. A scan will tell us.'

His eyes widened. 'The ball…the performance. We should cancel. You need to rest.'

She pulled back laughing. 'I'm pregnant. Not an invalid. We're playing together, and you're being formally announced as Special Advisor of State to His Highness. There is *no way* we're missing the ball.'

When she and Stefano had returned to Lasserno permanently, Alessio had reached out to suggest the role and Stefano had accepted. Not because of the weight of family history or any sense of obligation. Because it had been a deeply heartfelt offer from one friend to another.

Anyhow, Stefano was already a true Shield to the Crown. A protector at heart. He'd nurtured and protected her.

'So long as you're sure.'

He placed his warm hand on her stomach, looked deep into her eyes, and the emotion she witnessed there would have cut her off at the knees if she hadn't known he would always hold her up.

'I've never been surer of anything. I'm so proud of you, Stefano, and I want everyone to see how much.'

'You are the song in my life. The music in my heart. My love for you makes me better at everything I do. Yours are the only accolades I'll ever need.'

He bent, swung her high into his arms, and Lucy threw her head back, laughing at the happiness of yet another perfect moment.

'And now, *tesoro*, it's time for me to show you the stars again.'

* * * * *

COMING NEXT MONTH FROM

H HARLEQUIN

PRESENTS

#3985 BOUND BY HER RIVAL'S BABY
Ghana's Most Eligible Billionaires
by Maya Blake
Why, wonders Amelie, does she feel such a wild attraction to Atu? He wants to buy her family's beach resort, so he's completely off-limits. Yet surrendering to their heat was inevitable...and now she's pregnant with his heir!

#3986 THE ITALIAN'S RUNAWAY CINDERELLA
by Louise Fuller
Talitha's disappearance from his life has haunted billionaire Dante. Now he'll put their relationship on fresh footing—by hiring her to work for him. Yet with their chemistry as hot as ever, will he ever be able to let her go again?

#3987 FORBIDDEN TO THE POWERFUL GREEK
Cinderellas of Convenience
by Carol Marinelli
The secret to Galen's success is his laser-sharp focus. And young widow Roula is disruption personified! Most disruptive of all? The smoldering attraction he can't act on when he hires her as his temporary assistant!

#3988 CONSEQUENCES OF THEIR WEDDING CHARADE
by Cathy Williams
Jess doesn't know what she was thinking striking a just-for-show arrangement to accompany notorious playboy Curtis to an A-List wedding. What will the paparazzi uncover first—their charade...or that Jess is now expecting his baby?

HPCNMRA0122B

#3989 THE BILLIONAIRE'S LAST-MINUTE MARRIAGE

The Greeks' Race to the Altar

by Amanda Cinelli

With his first bride stolen at the altar, Greek CEO Xander needs a replacement, fast! Only his secretary Pandora—the woman he holds responsible for ruining his wedding day—will do... But her touch sparks unforeseen desire!

#3990 THE INNOCENT'S ONE-NIGHT PROPOSAL

by Jackie Ashenden

After everything cynical Castor has witnessed, there's almost nothing he's surprised by. But naive Glory's offer to sell him her virginity floors him! Of course, it's out of the question. Instead, he makes a counter-proposal: become his convenient bride!

#3991 THE COST OF THEIR ROYAL FLING

Princesses by Royal Decree

by Lucy Monroe

Prince Dimitri's mission to discover who's leaking palace secrets leads him to an incendiary fling with Jenna. As their connection deepens, could the truth cost him the only woman that sees beyond his royal title?

#3992 A DEAL FOR THE TYCOON'S DIAMONDS

The Infamous Cabrera Brothers

by Emmy Grayson

Anna has spent years healing from her former best friend Antonio's rejection. Then a dramatic fall into the billionaire's arms spark headlines. And his solution to refocus the unwanted attention? A ruse of a romance!

YOU CAN FIND MORE INFORMATION ON UPCOMING HARLEQUIN TITLES, FREE EXCERPTS AND MORE AT HARLEQUIN.COM.

HPCNMRB0122B

A breeze washed over Amelie and she shivered.

Within one moment and the next, Atu was shrugging off his shirt.

"Wh-what are you doing?" she blurted as he came toward her.

Another mirthless twist of his lips. "You may deem me an enemy, but I don't want you catching cold and falling ill. Or worse."

She aimed a glare his way. "Not until I've signed on whatever dotted line you're determined to foist on me, you mean?"

That look of fury returned. This time accompanied by a flash of disappointment. As if he had the right to such a lofty emotion where she was concerned. She wanted, no, *needed* to refuse this small offer of comfort.

To return to her room and come up with a definite plan that removed him from her life for good.

So why was she drawing the flaps of his shirt closer? Her fingers clinging to the warm cotton as if she'd never let it go?

She must have made a sound at the back of her throat, because his head swung toward her, his eyes holding hers for an age before he exhaled harshly.

His lips firmed and for a long stretch he didn't speak. "You need to accept that I'm the best bet you have right now. There's no use fighting. I'm going to win eventually. How soon depends entirely on you."

The implacable conclusion sent icy shivers coursing through her. In that moment she regretted every moment of weakness. Regretted feeling bad for invoking that hint of disappointment in his eyes.

She had nothing to be ashamed of. Not when vanquishing her and her family was his sole, true purpose.

She snatched his shirt from her shoulders, crushing her body's instant insistence on its warmth as she tossed it back to him. "You should know by now that threats don't faze me. We're still here, still standing after all you and your family have done. So go ahead, do your worst."

Head held high, she whirled away from him. She made it only three steps before he captured her wrist. She spun around, intent on pushing him away.

But that ruthlessness was coupled with something else. Something hot and blazing and all-consuming in his eyes.

She belatedly read it as lust before he was tugging her closer, wrapping one hand around her waist and the other in her hair. "This stubborn determination is admirable. Hell, I'd go so far as to say it's a turn-on, because God knows I admire strong, willful women," he muttered, his lips a hairsbreadth from hers, "but fiery passion will only get you so far."

"And what are you going to do about it?" she taunted a little too breathlessly. Every cell in her body traitorously strained toward him, yearning for things she knew she shouldn't want but desperately needed anyway.

He froze, then with a strangled sound leaving his throat, he slammed his lips onto hers.

He kissed her like he was starved for it. *For her.*

Don't miss
Bound by Her Rival's Baby,
available March 2022 wherever
Harlequin Presents books and ebooks are sold.

Harlequin.com

Get 4 FREE REWARDS!

We'll send you 2 FREE Books plus 2 FREE Mystery Gifts.

Harlequin Presents books feature the glamorous lives of royals and billionaires in a world of exotic locations, where passion knows no bounds.

FREE Value Over **$20**

HARLEQUIN

Heartfelt or thrilling, passionate or uplifting—Harlequin is more than just happily-ever-after.

With twelve different series to choose from and new books available every month, you are sure to find stories that will move you, uplift you, inspire and delight you.

SIGN UP FOR THE HARLEQUIN NEWSLETTER

Be the first to hear about great new reads and exciting offers!

Harlequin.com/newsletters